A
Harlequin
Romance

OTHER
Harlequin Romances
by HENRIETTA REID

1094—MY DARK RAPPAREE
1126—MAN OF THE ISLANDS
1206—SUBSTITUTE FOR LOVE
1247—LAIRD OF STORR
1317—BELOVED SPARROW
1380—RELUCTANT MASQUERADE
1430—HUNTER'S MOON
1460—THE BLACK DELANEY
1495—RIVAL SISTERS
1528—THE MADE MARRIAGE
1575—SISTER OF THE BRIDE
1621—GARTH OF TREGILLIS
1720—INTRUDER AT WINDGATES

Many of these titles are available at your local bookseller
or through the Harlequin Reader Service.

For a free catalogue listing all available Harlequin Romances,
send your name and address to:

HARLEQUIN READER SERVICE,
M.P.O. Box 707, Niagara Falls, N.Y. 14302
Canadian address: Stratford, Ontario, Canada.

or use order coupon at back of book.

INTRUDER
AT WINDGATES

by

HENRIETTA REID

HARLEQUIN BOOKS   TORONTO
WINNIPEG

Original hard cover edition published in 1973
by Mills & Boon Limited

© Henrietta Reid 1973

SBN 373-01720-0

Harlequin edition published September 1973

1720   Printed in Canada

CHAPTER I

'A few more minutes and we'll be in Kirtleside,' the stout party in the corner of the carriage informed Jane.

'Oh! I didn't realise we were so near.' Jane Talbot sprang to her feet.

She had been chatting to the woman who was her only companion for the past half hour and had not noticed how quickly time had passed. She glanced at herself in the small mirror let into the upper part of the side of the compartment, adjusted the small crocheted beret on her soft brown curls, smoothed the collar of her rumpled blouse and drew on her gloves. What would Aunt Ellen think of her? she wondered a little nervously. They had not met since she was a child and Aunt Ellen Ferguson had been notorious in her family for her critical and arbitrary opinions.

As the train slid slowly along the platform and 'Kirtleside' appeared on the broad noticeboard, she reached up and pulled down her soft travelling bags from the rack, then stepped down on to the platform, to find that she was the only passenger getting off at the station.

The friendly stout lady leaned out of the window. 'Has no one come to meet you?' she inquired solicitously, scanning the platform and the wide gravelled yard outside. 'Oh, but wait a minute! Perhaps this is for you.' She pointed to a small blue car which at that moment was being driven into the yard.

It slewed to a halt and a thin young man with bright red hair sprang out and hurried towards the luggage compartment at the end of the train.

At that moment too, Jane awoke to the fact that a rather elderly and dismal-looking porter was standing at her elbow. 'And where are you for?' he inquired in lugubrious tones.

'Windgates,' Jane answered.

The porter scratched his head and looked about vaguely. 'Well, there's no conveyance for you from Windgates,' he remarked helplessly.

'Perhaps I could walk,' Jane suggested doubtfully. Dimly she recollected that Great-aunt Ferguson's home had seemed to be in the heart of the country, miles away from the station. But then she had been only a child on her last visit and perhaps the distances had seemed greater than they really were.

'It would be a sight too far in them shoes,' the porter pronounced, glancing down at Jane's sandals. 'But perhaps the doctor will give you a lift. Well, there's no harm in trying at any rate.' As he spoke, he lifted her bags and moved off along the platform towards the luggage van where the red-haired young man was busily superintending the unloading of a cardboard box, punched with air-holes, from which issued a continual cheeping sound, as if it were full of hungry fledglings.

'Where's the part for McIntyre's tractor?' the young man demanded a little irritably, before the porter could begin his plea.

'Oh, it'll be there somewhere, you may be sure. You just bide there a wee and I'll look it out for you. You wouldn't think of giving this young lady a lift to Windgates when you're dropping by McIntyre's, would you?' he inquired.

'Windgates?'

Jane found herself fixed by a pair of very observant, bright blue eyes. And this, combined with the thin, lean build and the red hair, gave her the distinct impression that she had arrived in the Highlands at last.

'They didnae send a car for her, poor soul,' the porter told him, 'and we were wondering if you'd take her as far as Windgates, for she's no got the shoes on her for a long walk.'

'Just typical of the set-up at Windgates,' the young doctor said grimly, as he hoisted the cardboard box carefully and began to walk towards the small blue car. Jane followed meekly. He opened the passenger door. 'Hop in. You're very welcome, but this will give you a taste of what you're in for. If I were you I'd turn right around and go back home, young lady. But then I suppose the pay is good and that has to be taken into consideration!'

Jane stared at him in amazement, but he was unaware of her reaction as he placed the cardboard box carefully on the back seat. The sweet cheeping sound issued without cessation. Then he hoisted her luggage into the boot and when the old porter had arrived with McIntyre's tractor part, the red-headed young man got in beside her.

'I'd better introduce myself,' he said as he started the car. 'I'm Gregory Shields, professionally doctor to the community, but in fact, general handyman, as you can see for yourself. Anyone who's too busily engaged otherwise sends me to the station to fetch parts of tractors, etc., as soon as they hear I'm to collect a box of day-old chicks for myself.'

'So that's what they are!' Jane exclaimed, glancing back at the cardboard box. 'I was wondering what that cheeping sound was.'

'You didn't think it was a box of canaries?' he asked with a flash of white teeth.

'I didn't know what it was,' Jane admitted. 'Although I knew it must be birds of some kind, of course. But are you sure the poor little things aren't smothering in that cardboard box?' she asked, eying it a little anxiously.

'Oh no, there's no chance of that,' he assured her. 'Besides, air is not a commodity that chicks care a lot about anyway. They don't get much of it in their natural environment, which would be sheltering under the hen's feathers for the first few hours of their lives.'

'But what about food and water?' Jane asked. 'Surely they must be desperately thirsty?'

'Wrong again,' he informed her. 'And really, my dear young lady, these questions are a giveaway; they speak volumes as to your ignorance of everything concerning country life. Chickens neither eat nor drink during the first twenty-four hours of their lives, and that's why we have them transported as day-old chicks so that the journey will be as easy as possible for them.'

'Oh!' Jane felt a little at a loss.

'Yes. Oh,' he told her. 'Is that all you have to say?'

'Well, yes, I admit I'm ignorant as far as day-old chicks are concerned,' Jane said a little defensively. 'But I see you're a real countryman.'

He nodded as they drove out of the station yard. 'I really like country life and I don't believe I'd ever be happy or contented anywhere else. My father was doctor here at Kirtleside and as soon as I qualified I returned here to take over from him. Although it was a pity he retired, because he didn't live very long afterwards. I think it was mainly because he felt he was useless, no longer at everyone's beck and call. Now I've full responsibility here—not that I'm too busy, I must admit. People around here are depressingly healthy, much too vigorous to make any doctor rich, so it's as well I can turn my hand to country pursuits and I must say I like it this way. I'm able occasionally when the skies are right to put " Gone fishing" on my door and go off for the day when I choose.'

Jane glanced at him. His healthy freckled appearance and the reddish-orange tone of his skin bespoke the man who spent a lot of his time outdoors.

' But enough about me,' he went on. ' I'll admit I'm curious to know just what you're doing in this part of the world.'

' I'm Jane Talbot, and I'm going to stay with my aunt, Ellen Ferguson.'

' Ellen Ferguson! '

There was surprise in his tone and she added instantly, ' Well, great-aunt really, although I never called her that or think of her that way.'

There was silence in the car for a long moment and she was aware of his swift assessing glance before he said, ' I thought you had probably come for a completely different reason.'

She looked at him in surprise, but he didn't elaborate and went on rather hurriedly as though to prevent further questions, ' Your aunt has not been keeping too well recently. She's showing her age for one reason and another.'

' I haven't seen her for years,' Jane admitted, ' although I've had an open invitation for a long time.'

9

A shade crossed her face as she remembered the reason why she had at last decided to make the journey to Scotland. Her father had married again, and the fact was that she and her new stepmother didn't get along in the big Victorian house on the outskirts of London.

Gregory Shields glanced at her briefly. 'So you haven't seen her for some time? In that case you'll notice the changes even more than I do.'

'Oh, I had a letter from her some time ago. We've always kept in touch, but I haven't visited Kirtleside since I was a child. I could hardly remember it—except that it was surrounded by mountains and moors and was very beautiful.'

'Yes, Kirtleside is very beautiful, I agree, but I think you should prepare yourself for surprises,' he said enigmatically.

'Well, one thing I don't expect to find changed—at least not in character—is Aunt Ellen,' Jane laughed. 'She was always so very forthright and outspoken. In fact, I remember I was rather afraid of her when I was a child.'

'Oh, she's still as outspoken as ever. But I think you'll find she's greatly changed in other ways,' he said slowly. 'It's not altogether surprising, considering recent events.'

'What events?' Jane asked, startled.

'You mean, she didn't mention the matter in her letters?' he asked cautiously.

'Except that she seemed to have a sort of feud on with someone called Morris Leslie. She didn't go into details and it was all a little confusing, but then she always did seem to have a feud on with someone or other, so I didn't take much notice, but I can see from your manner that this must be something quite serious.'

He seemed about to reply, then, as the car approached the great gates with ' Windgates ' written in gold lettering on the piers, he slowed and edged into the avenue before he said, ' Ellen Ferguson is a proud woman, as no doubt you already know. She's extremely self-willed. If she hasn't told you of her troubles in her letters, then I'm sure she would resent my discussing her business. Better to hear it all from her own lips. However, I can tell you this much, this is no ordinary quarrel, and for once she's finding herself on the losing side.'

Slowly the car moved along the drive towards the house and as they came around a curve in the avenue she recognised it as being the same as it had been in her childhood: a tall, flat-fronted house built of blocks of granite, with rather small windows, it rose sheer out of the ground, just as she remembered it, and instantly she thought how uncompromisingly dour it looked. Somehow one never saw houses like this in England. Then as she glanced through a gate let into a wall she drew in her breath in delight at the beauty of the scene that met her gaze; it was a lovely walled garden, in the centre of which was a patch of smooth velvet lawn where a fountain was playing. In great broad beds around the walls were masses of spring flowers; daffodils and narcissi, forsythia and crocus were in abundance, so that the view through the wrought-iron gate was of one delightful blaze of colour.

Nearer the house gardeners were setting out beds of wallflowers: aubretia tumbled in purple and white masses from ornamental urns and against the side of the house was a giant conservatory, inside which she could glimpse delicately shaded carnations and banks of giant white lilies. In growing amazement Jane realised that the whole atmosphere of the place was one of wealth in abundance. Yet more than once Aunt Ellen had hinted of straitened means in her letters. The conservatory, for instance! Jane wrinkled her brow in the effort to remember if it had been there when she had last visited Windgates. Perhaps it had existed then, perhaps it had not been noticeable then because it was shabby, the frames broken and the paint discoloured. But now it blazed with white paint and was obviously filled with choice blooms.

'Hope you don't mind my dumping you now,' Gregory Shields remarked as he extracted her luggage from the boot, 'but young Tommy Phillipson has measles and I'd better call in on him before I go home. See you around!' And with a perfunctory wave he drove off.

Left to herself, Jane was struck by the air of affluence that seemed to envelop the place like an aura. It was obvious that this was an establishment that was kept in perfect order with no regard to expense, and it accorded ill with the faint hints Aunt Ellen had let fall in her letters and also with the suggestion of pity in the young doctor's tone when he had spoken of her. The whole tone of the place was so different from her memories of it that for a moment the bizarre thought crossed her mind that she had come to the wrong house. This was only a stupid idea, of course, she thought as, troubled, she approached the narrow door set right in the middle of the high building and tapped with the ornate brass knocker which winked in the early summer sunlight.

There was no reply to her knocking and then she spotted the electric press bell. She touched this and shortly a neat maid in a well-fitting dark blue-and-white striped overall opened the door.

In response to the slight expression of inquiry on the girl's pretty face Jane said, ' I'm Jane Talbot.'

The girl's expression cleared. ' Oh yes, I'm sure the master's expecting you. If you follow me I'll show you into the library.'

The master! What on earth did the girl mean? Jane wondered.

In bewildered silence she followed the girl across the shining floor of the hall and entered the room, the door of which the girl held open for her. And here Jane's mystification increased a hundredfold because this was the room which on her former visit to Windgates had been the big living-room for the family. Now it was altered out of all recognition. Then her eyes fell upon the great chimneypiece and immediately she felt reassured to see the familiar carving in the stone. Yet, even here, difference had been introduced, because the intricate pattern had been touched up skilfully by a master hand and the scars inflicted by the pokers of generations of children had been eradicated.

Before she had time to ask the girl any questions, Jane found herself alone in the great room and examined it at her leisure. There was plenty to interest her. Snowy sheepskin rugs were spread on the shining parquet floor. The furniture was upholstered in leather of a pale beige shade and a wide brass-bound table which obviously served for a desk stood slantwise to the bright fire that burned upon the hearth. A beautifully carved circular staircase led off from one corner of the room to a gallery in which was stored leather and gilt bound books. Attached to the walls were stags' heads and the occasional tables were loaded with bibelots of obvious value. In the corners and here and there along the walls were suits of armour and ancient weapons. Bemused, Jane wandered about the great room, stopping to stare at the pieces of rare old Scottish silver displayed upon an occasional table. She stopped before an array of claymores attached to one of the walls. This was not at all like Aunt Ellen's beloved Victorian vases, the Dresden shepherdesses, the carved bureaux and oval burr walnut tables, the crystal girandoles with their glinting prisms that caught the sun, splintering it into a myriad scintillating lights.

She moved about, puzzling about the strange meta-morphosis in the old home. Was it possible Aunt Ellen had married—at her age—and had not mentioned it in any of her letters? If so, she had certainly married a wealthy man. And why was it Aunt Ellen had not come to welcome her, but was obviously leaving her to be greeted first by 'the master'. But how extra-ordinary to think of the acrimonious Aunt Ellen marry-ing! The idea seemed utterly fantastic, she had seemed such a confirmed old maid, Jane was thinking. It would be typical of her to leave out any mention of it in her letters and surprise her.

It was at this point that the door opened and Jane swung around to find that a tall woman in a neat dress of dark blue—the same shade of blue as the maid's striped overall, Jane noted almost absently—was stand-ing in the doorway. She was carrying a beautiful ornate tray upon which gleamed a silver service. 'I'm Mrs MacInnes, the housekeeper. The master has been delayed. He's overseeing the work in the plantations, so I've brought you some tea. No doubt you'll be needing it after your journey,' she told Jane with a smile.

As the woman placed the tray upon an occasional table and began to poke the already blazing fire Jane seized upon the opportunity to question her. 'The master always insists on a fire,' the housekeeper was saying. 'You'd need it in this part of the country no matter what the weather's like.'

'Where is my aunt?' Jane demanded more sharply than she had intended, but tension had been building up almost unbearably.

'Your aunt?' The woman straightened and looked at her inquiringly.

'Yes, Miss Ferguson, Miss Ellen Ferguson,' Jane said almost feverishly.

'And is she your aunt? My now, isn't that a coincidence?' she exclaimed, regarding Jane with interest.

'Yes. When am I to see her?' Jane demanded.

'Oh, Mrs Ferguson is very seldom here,' the woman replied. 'The master and Mrs Ferguson don't see eye to eye, more's the pity!'

'What do you mean?' Jane burst out.

'Well, I don't think it's my place to discuss these things—especially as you've only arrived,' the woman told her with a hint of reproof. 'The master is a good employer, very considerate, and pays good wages, but he can be strict too, and he doesn't like his business to be discussed by the staff. You'd better bring this up with himself when he comes in. As for me, I have fine quarters here with my own suite of rooms with TV and every comfort, and I don't intend to jeopardise my future by gossiping about what doesn't concern me.'

'But who is this person you call " the master "?' Jane burst out in exasperation.

'Why, Mr Morris Leslie, of course, who else would it be?'

And with this, a rather huffy expression on her face, the housekeeper went out and closed the door after her.

Jane poured out a cup of tea because she was very thirsty, but she was unable to touch the dainty cucumber sandwiches or the cakes, oozing rich cream and chocolate. She felt as if to eat would choke her. Now her fears were fully aroused. What had happened to Aunt Ellen and the conviction that she was in some dreadful predicament filled her mind with foreboding. For an instant her impulse was to rush out of the house, but a stubborn streak in her character made her hold her ground. She would not budge from this place until the mystery was cleared up, she resolved.

After what seemed an age, but was no more than half an hour according to the bracket clock hung on the wall near the chimneypiece, the door was flung open and Jane swung around to find herself being stared at by a man who was striding across the room towards her. Her first impression was of extreme vitality. Even before she felt the pressure of his hand in the warm handshake which accompanied his words of apology for keeping her waiting.

'Please sit down,' he invited as he moved on to take his place behind the big desk. 'I'm usually at home at this time, but today I was unfortunately detained at the plantations.'

There could be no reply to this and immediately he went on, 'But of course this is all Greek to you. You could have no knowledge of what alterations are being planned here. Now let me see, if I remember correctly you stated that your shorthand and typing are excellent. You are also able to take responsibility—but then you must be when you've been able to hold down such a position of trust for so many years. By the way, you look rather younger than I would have expected from your description of your business experience. However, your qualifications are excellent and—'

While he had been speaking he had rapidly been riffling through the papers on his desk and now held up a letter. 'Yes, here's your letter of application. And as I said, you'd need to be able to make decisions on your own, because my time is fully occupied at present. Windgates was in pretty poor shape when I came into it and I intend to turn it into a fully paying proposition. Now as to salary—'

'Just a minute,' cried Jane. 'What have you done with my aunt?'

There was a lengthy silence while the man across the desk stared at her intently and she had time to note the shock of thick dark hair and the general air of vitality and strength in his mobile, regular features.

'I'm sure I must have misunderstood you,' he said after a moment, 'but I thought I heard you asking what had I done with your aunt.'

'Yes, that's what I said, what have you done with her?' Jane demanded.

'When I invited you to come for an interview I had no idea you expected to meet your aunt here,' he said with heavy sarcasm. 'In fact when I employ a young lady as my secretary I rarely expect her aunt to turn up also.'

'But I didn't answer any advertisement,' cried Jane, springing to her feet in alarm. 'I'm not here to be interviewed. I'm here to see my aunt, and I won't go away until I find out what's become of her.'

He regarded her impassively for a long moment and again riffled through a bundle of papers and produced a letter which he glanced at frowningly. 'Then I take it that you are not Miss Rhoda Mannering whose shorthand and typing are so excellent and who has held down a position of responsibility for many years and who now wishes a change of occupation and would like to work in the country.'

'I'm Jane Talbot, and I've come to see my aunt, Miss Ellen Ferguson, who lives here. I won't be put off any longer. I demand an explanation!' Jane replied with rising panic.

'Do be seated, Miss Talbot,' he said, a note of exasperation in his tone. 'I see that we're under a complete misunderstanding. Perhaps we'd better go back to the beginning and start again. And I advise you to pour yourself a cup of tea and be calm, for to begin with I've done nothing whatsoever with your aunt except to pay her a very good price indeed for her home, and to establish her in what was formerly the factor's house—not, I may say, that that prevents her regarding me as her worst enemy. Her enmity plagues me—or would do so if I permitted myself to be disturbed by that sort of thing.'

Jane felt her knees tremble beneath her, and sank into the chair in front of the desk. 'You—you mean that Aunt Ellen no longer lives here?'

He nodded grimly, his brows forming a thick straight line across his tanned forehead. 'Exactly! As I mentioned, I gave your aunt a fair price for Windgates, but in spite of that she behaves as if I had robbed her.' His mouth twisted sardonically. 'Obviously she sees me as a sort of robber baron, intent on bullying lone ladies into parting with their property at the point of the sword.' He leaned back in his chair and surveyed her thoughtfully. 'By the way, I don't know if you're aware of the fact, but your aunt was in what I might tactfully describe as straitened circumstances when I appeared on the scene. The house was up for sale and I bought it; a business transaction. It's as simple as that, yet, as I say, she behaves as if she had been evicted at sword point. By the way,' he interjected abruptly, ' why don't you pour tea? You look as if you could do with some refreshment.'

In silence and with trembling hands Jane did as she was told. There was something about this man that seemed to demand obedience. She picked up the ornate silver teapot and half filled the delicate china cup and was grateful for the warm golden liquid. Somehow it gave her strength to face again this dark, grim-faced man and the knowledge that her aunt no longer owned Windgates.

She was aware of being watched keenly as she sipped.

' Well, feel better?'

She nodded silently. Then, laying down her cup, was appalled to hear it rattle in the saucer. Instantly, she knew that to this man she must show no signs of weakness. She tilted her head defiantly.

' Perhaps I was wrong in advising refreshments,' he said dryly. ' If I'm not mistaken I see the light of battle in those extraordinarily blue eyes of yours.'

' I'm afraid I'm not quite satisfied with your explanation,' Jane said stiffly.

' And what further explanation do you want, Miss Talbot?' He put two broad hands on the arms of his chair and stood up. ' What on earth am I expected to say that will satisfy you?' He began to pace the room with long impatient strides. ' As I have already told you, she now lives in what I believe in former days was called the factor's house, and may I add I was under no onus to supply her with alternative accommodation. I should advise you to keep that in mind.'

Jane laughed shortly and with a hint of triumph said, 'You have obviously overlooked one thing, Mr Leslie, with your talk of providing " alternative accommodation ".'

He drew to a stop in front of her. 'And what might that be, Miss Talbot?' he asked mockingly.

'You are obviously unaware that as a child I stayed at Windgates, and I remember the factor's house—a broken-down ruin, in fact. I used often to play there. The windows and doors were broken and the roof almost caved in. It was no doubt a splendid place for a child to play in, but completely uninhabitable. How dare you pretend you're doing my aunt a favour by letting her stay in that derelict old house!' Her voice choked with rage.

'I see,' he said musingly, 'that I've got another antagonist on my hands.'

'You most certainly have!' she said fiercely, springing to her feet.

There was only one thing she desired now and that was to be out of this odious man's presence. She snatched up her bag and gloves and headed for the door.

'I'll see your luggage is carried over to the factor's house,' he said easily. 'By the way, would you like me to accompany you or will you find your own way?'

'You forget I've already told you I stayed here as a child,' she snapped. 'I can easily find my own way, thanks.'

He stood with his back to the fire and shrugged. 'Very well, just as you wish, but might I remind you that there have been several changes here, as no doubt you have already noticed, so don't be surprised if the old landmarks have been obliterated.'

She stared at him blankly for a moment. What on earth did he mean? she wondered, then turning wrenched open the door and slammed it decisively behind her.

The hall was deserted and for a moment she contemplated her heavy suitcases piled in a corner. It would have given her great satisfaction to have removed them immediately herself, she thought, and be under no obligation to this odious man. Then she remembered the long walk to the factor's house and realised how impossible it would be.

She hurried past the gables and down the long path that led to the old house, still seething with anger.

Poor Aunt Ellen! Jane felt her heart ache with a mixture of pity and anger. She had always been her own worst enemy! Instead of husbanding her inheritance she had fecklessly indulged in expensive litigation with her neighbours and with those who might have proved her friends.

Gradually, as she gained control of her emotions, Jane halted uncertainly. Surely, although it was so many years since she had come this way, she should have remembered the narrow overgrown path with its bracken and briers. But this was a broad, well-tended path edged with box. She stopped, wondering if she should retrace her steps, but curiosity led her on. She approached a broad, sweeping turn. If she was not mistaken the narrow track had twisted in somewhat the same way, hiding the house from sight until one came on it suddenly.

She rounded the bend in the broad path and stood bemused. A house was plainly in sight, but it certainly wasn't the old ruins which had always been called 'the factor's house'. This was a split-level bungalow-type house with wide picture windows. Slowly she went forward, and then she spotted Ellen Ferguson in the wide lawn that stretched from the windows to meet the broad driveway which ran past the house. Ellen Ferguson was watering the flowers in the herbaceous border which ran as a colourful background to the lawn.

'Aunt Ellen!' Jane exclaimed and, breaking into a run, raced across the lawn towards the elderly woman.

Ellen Ferguson stopped, watering-can in hand. 'Just as well you're not wearing high heels, young woman,' she said severely. 'I never permit anyone to prod holes in my lawn. And who are you, anyway?'

Jane stopped and drew back, embarrassed. Now that she was close to the stooped figure she was appalled at the change in Ellen Ferguson. This was not the upright, forceful woman whom she remembered since her visit to Kirtleside as a child. This was an old lady with an unmistakable air of frailty. Only the eyes were still bright and challenging.

'Don't you know me, Aunt?' she stammered. 'I'm Jane, Jane Talbot.'

'Jane! So you've come at last, after all these years!' Ellen Ferguson said gruffly. But she put down the watering-can and folded Jane in her arms. 'You're welcome, even if you've put me off from year to year, always promising to come and never doing it. You've grown.'

'It's not surprising,' Jane laughed a little shakily. 'One does in twenty years.'

'True,' the old lady said, 'but somehow I've always pictured you as you were.'

And I have always remembered you as I saw you last, Jane might have told her, gazing at that emaciated, stooped figure.

'And now we must have some tea,' her aunt said decisively, leading the way towards the house.

Jane was now forced to admit that she had just had tea.

'Well, I want mine,' the old lady said a little crossly as she led the way into a spotless modern kitchen and plugged in an electric kettle.

'I've a very good woman, Maggie Crampsie, who comes in each morning to help me,' Ellen Ferguson told her as she set a cup and saucer on a tea trolley and took cake from a tin.

As the kettle boiled Ellen Ferguson spooned tea into the stainless steel teapot with a generous hand while Jane looked about in amazement. One thing was abundantly clear, and that was that the factor's house must have been completely pulled down and this shining modern house built in its stead: nothing was now left of the old factor's house but the name.

When everything was ready Jane assisted her aunt to push the tea-trolley into the spacious sitting-room with wood block floors and wide picture windows, where Jane found at last something that she remembered from the past. And that was the furniture and orna-ments. Instantly she remembered the girandoles glitter-ing on a marble-topped table. On the mantelshelf stood the French clock and the Sèvres vases. The gleaming mahogany table was the same one Aunt Ellen had used so many years ago. It was strange to see these old-world pieces established here in this modern room.

As she sipped tea Ellen Ferguson questioned her niece closely. 'And how did you travel?' she asked.

'By plane, I suppose! Horrid dangerous things. It will be a long time before you see me in one of those things.'

Jane told her she had come by train.

'But that was in hours ago. I may lead a secluded life here, but I know what time the trains get in.' Ellen Ferguson eyed her suspiciously over the rim of her china cup.

Somehow or other Jane knew that her aunt would be none too pleased to know that she had spent her time in the home of the new owner of Windgates. 'The doctor drove me from the station,' she replied evasively, hoping to head her off.

'Oh, young Gregory,' Ellen snorted. 'He's a fine young fellow, but not the doctor his father was—nor ever will be. Those tablets he's giving me for these headaches of mine aren't doing me a bit of good. "Keep them up," he says. So I've kept them up, but I see no improvement whatsoever, so now I simply take a few out of the bottle every day and chuck them away. No use filling yourself up with muck if it isn't doing you any good.'

Jane couldn't help smiling as she watched her aunt pour herself another cup of tea. She guessed that Gregory Shields had his hands full with Aunt Ellen for a patient.

'Still, being driven by Gregory Shields doesn't account for your turning up at this time of the day,' Ellen Ferguson returned to the attack.

'Well, I went to Windgates,' Jane told her. 'Naturally—'

'Yes, naturally you thought you'd find me there,' Ellen broke in. 'But instead you found that man installed in my old home.'

'But—but he tells me it was up for sale,' Jane interposed. 'You didn't tell me you were thinking of selling the old house. I knew you were so fond of it. It's been in the family for so long, hasn't it?'

She fancied there was a touch of embarrassment in her aunt's face as she lowered it in a pretence of breaking a biscuit. 'Yes, I intended to let you know, but there was no need for me to tell you that Windgates had been sold because, living in the grounds, naturally your letters would always find me.'

Jane gazed across at the old face now meeting her glance a little defiantly.

It was only too plain what Aunt Ellen had had in mind. It was true that up until now she had not availed herself of her aunt's invitation and no doubt the old woman had begun to believe that she would never do so. Ellen Ferguson's fierce pride in her home and her old possessions had made her keep the news of the great change in her way of life from those in London. The years might have passed and Jane's letters to Miss Ellen Ferguson, Windgates, Kirtleside would still have found their way to the old woman. Her pride would have been wounded by having to admit that she had had to sell the family house which had belonged to the Fergusons for hundreds of years. But this admission somehow made the old lady's position all the more poignant.

'So you went to Windgates and found that young interloper in my place,' Ellen Ferguson returned to her grievance. 'Would you believe it, Jane, that man bought Windgates simply out of revenge.'

'Revenge?' Jane gazed at her in amazement.

'Yes, revenge! At first it looked like an ordinary sale. And I admit it *was* up for sale, but why do you think Morris Leslie set his heart on it?'

'Because he liked it,' Jane suggested weakly.

'Nonsense,' her aunt rejoined stoutly. 'If he had liked it why would he instantly set about changing everything? Had I known at the time what he intended to do with it I should never have let him have it. I'd rather it had fallen down in ruins about my head. It turns out that he is descended from the Leslie family who were put out in the time of the clearances. As you know, after the Jacobite rising of 1745 all over the Highlands the crofters were put off their holdings and their land given over to the raising of sheep. Well, it transpires that Morris Leslie is descended from one of those who were turned off their land here at Kirtleside and emigrated to Canada. Evidently he was brought up to feel bitterness about it, so what does the young jackanapes do but come along, now that the family have done well in Canada, and buy the Ferguson family home so that he can crow it over the last of the family to whom his ancestors were once beholden.'

Jane gazed at her in dismay. How much truth was there in this? she wondered. Ellen Ferguson was a woman who needed someone to feud with, if life was to be interesting. Had she simply picked on the new-comer as the handiest person to battle with in her old age?

'Oh, you needn't look at me as if I were havering,' Aunt Ellen said with acerbity. 'I know it's true. First of all he admitted his family were dispossessed by the Fergusons—not, of course, that he admits that his motive is malicious, but I'm not deluded enough to think that Windgates is a particularly beautiful or desirable home. As I've told you, he's wealthy. There were plenty of much more attractive properties up for sale. Why did he have to choose Windgates of all places to settle in when he could have afforded to buy any home he set his heart on? No, you can take my word for it, Morris Leslie's motive in buying Windgates was revenge pure and simple.'

Could Aunt Ellen be right in her estimate of the new owner's motives? Jane wondered. The idea struck cold to her heart. It was quite possible, of course. It would not be easy to define the motives of the enigmatic man who now possessed Windgates.

A glance around the room they were seated in brought her a certain degree of reassurance. At least her aunt was comfortable in this bright modern house with every convenience to make life easy for her in her old age, and with all her little treasures around her to remind her of the days gone by.

'This house isn't too bad,' Jane ventured. 'You know, when he told me you were living in the house we used to call "the factor's house", I pictured it as it used to be and I felt so worried about you. When I turned the bend in the new drive and saw how completely changed everything was, I was delighted.'

'Were you delighted indeed?' Ellen Ferguson sniffed. 'It's clear that you haven't yet taken a good look at the view from this window.' As she spoke she stood up and moved towards the giant picture window which constituted almost one side of the room. 'Just look at that,' she commanded with a wave of her hand, and Jane, gazing out over the majestic view before her, caught her breath as she saw what troubled her aunt. From this spot there was a breathtaking view over miles of moorland, loch and mountain, but in the middle distance the eye was disturbed by a great, livid gash cut into a plantation of conifers.

Here the trees had been slashed, and the vegetation cut away, so that a great bald patch from which tree stumps protruded caught the eye.

'And that is the spot where this vandal proposes to build chalets, where sportsmen can come and fish and shoot over the moors at their leisure. No doubt they will think how delightfully Scottish it is, but what about me? Am I to gaze out of my window at ghastly pink and blue concrete abominations spattered about the countryside, the place riddled with foreigners all shooting away like madmen so that we're afraid to put our noses out of doors?' Ellen Ferguson demanded.

As Jane gazed out on the scene, beautiful and peaceful except for that great barren patch which quite ruined the view and drew the eye with its ugliness, she felt something of the indignation that filled the older woman. 'How could he do such a thing?' she breathed. 'Why, it will spoil Kirtleside. Already the place is quite different—and when a whole colony of houses are built there it will be absolutely horrible.'

'Exactly,' Ellen Ferguson nodded grimly as she led the way back to the tea table. 'I wouldn't mind so much, mind you, if he were building houses for the people of the district. But to think that all this is being done for foreigners so that they can come here for a few months in the year and enjoy the sport and then go off again, leaving us to face this eyesore for the rest of our lives. A vandal and a philistine!' she exclaimed fiercely. 'Had I known what he had in mind I'd never have sold to him, but he plagued me until I gave way. And don't tell me that it isn't another deliberate campaign on his part to get revenge for his family being sent into exile during the clearances.'

'But that's so long ago, Aunt Ellen,' cried Jane.

'It's ridiculous to suppose that—'

'Is it so ridiculous?' her aunt interposed. 'We Scots have long memories. The motive of revenge has always played a large part with us. We save things up for years and then strike. Oh, no, it's not beyond the bounds of possibility by a long shot. You'd know yourself what I'm up against if you heard him speak of the history of his family and of the injuries they suffered at the hands of the Fergusons. To think that I have to endure this in my old age when I'm no longer able to give as good as I get. If I'd any money left I'd sue him for spoiling the scenic beauties of the valley. But of course he didn't pay me enough to permit me to move hand or foot. I can barely live on the little income from the capital I have from the sale of the house.'

Irresistibly now Jane found her eye drawn to the scene beyond the great picture window spoiled by that savage gash across the valley. She felt depression fall upon her. All her life she had held in her heart and treasured the memory of the beauty of Kirtleside. Now it was all spoiled. Only too clearly did she see her aunt's point of view. Ellen Ferguson had good cause to hate Morris Leslie.

CHAPTER II

In the morning Jane woke up and looked around with delight at the guest room which was now hers; it looked so spick and span with built-in wardrobes and modern teak furniture with straight, clean lines that pleased the eye. The coverlet on the bed was of marigold yellow, as were the gay cushions in the easy chair, a splash of colour against the pale ivory of the rest of the room.

She went to one of the windows and leaning out was in time to see a woman come along the path and disappear around the side of the house: soon a clattering and crashing sound from downstairs announced that breakfast was being prepared.

Later she went softly downstairs to find in the kitchen a sturdily-built woman stirring a saucepan of porridge. This would be Maggie Crampsie, Jane surmised.

'That smells delicious,' she said with a smile.

'Yes, and tastes it too,' Maggie told her uncompromisingly. 'No one makes better porridge in the district than Maggie Crampsie, though I do say so. You'll be the great-niece, new arrived from London?'

'That's right,' Jane answered as she seated herself at the kitchen table with its bright red shining work surface, and the woman put a bowl of porridge before her and pushed forward a shaker of salt and a big jug of creamy milk.

Jane poured in milk and then looked around the table.

'And what's missing?' Maggie Crampsie asked sharply.

'Sugar for the porridge,' Jane answered.

'Dear me, I've never heard of anyone using sugar with porridge before,' the woman said doubtfully.

'We English people do,' Jane told her with a smile. 'I remember how shocked everyone here was when I asked for sugar with my porridge when I was a child.'

But the woman wasn't particularly interested in the eating habits of the English. 'Are you staying long?' she asked, her eyes darting curiosity.

' Well, that depends—' Jane evaded an answer.

' Depends on how well you get on with old Miss Crosspatch,' Maggie answered shrewdly. ' She's a hard woman to get on with and no mistake. And what did you do in England? What did you work at?'

Jane was surprised at the tone the woman was adopting towards her employer. After all, if she disliked Aunt Ellen so much, why work for her, but she answered civilly, ' I was a typist—in the typists' pool.'

' Typists' pool,' the woman gave a short laugh. ' Well, that's something new to me. Do you swim about in it, by any chance?'

Jane smiled. Yes, no doubt to this woman who had probably spent her whole life in the Highlands of Scotland the life she had lived in London would seem unbelievably strange. Vividly she recollected the rush for the Tube in the morning, the clatter of the machines in the big room where she had worked with so many others. Then out to lunch. Back again in the afternoon, and then the rush for the Tube again and the return to the big Victorian house. That had been the happiest time of the day for her—until her stepmother had come upon the scene and changed everything so drastically, with her open enmity and fierce possessiveness.

' Have you any brothers or sisters?' Maggie broke in on her thoughts.

Silently Jane shook her head.

' Your father and mother alive?' persisted the woman.

' My father's alive,' Jane told her.

' And your mother?'

Again Jane shook her head.

' And is your father all on his own there in London?' Maggie asked, all curiosity. ' I thought you said you didn't know how long you were staying. Who's taking care of him while you're away?'

'He's not alone,' Jane told her. 'He has married again and my stepmother is with him.'

'Oh, so that's it.' Satisfied, the woman turned again to the big gleaming stove and began to make tea. 'It's the old, old story. The new stepmother doesn't get on with the grown-up daughter. You're hoping the old woman will take you in—and leave her little bit of money to you in due course, no doubt!'

What a horrible woman she was, Jane was thinking. How could Aunt Ellen bear to employ her? Then she reflected that it was perhaps difficult to get domestic help in this sparsely populated part of the country. It also struck her that Ellen Ferguson could be extremely sharp-tongued when she chose and had perhaps earned this woman's enmity.

'You'll maybe get a job typing with the new owner at Windgates,' the daily woman said as she placed upon the table a small stainless steel teapot and matching sugar bowl and milk jug, and whipped some golden scones from the oven. 'He's making great changes here in Kirtleside and soon there will be work for all. Your great-aunt doesn't like the way things are going and will not hear a word of good spoken about Mr Leslie, but I can tell you that a bit of employment around here would do no harm. When I was growing up there was nothing to do except emigrate to Glasgow, and many a girl from the Highlands pined away in the slums of the city, pinching and scraping and working from dawn to dark to send home the few pence to the family here in the North.'

As she spoke she placed a dish of curled butter pats on the table and a plate of rashers and eggs.

'Oh no, I daren't say a word of this to Miss Ferguson. I'd be sure to lose my job—not that the pittance she pays me would keep me here! If it weren't for the fact that Mr Leslie slips me a few extra quid from time to time Ellen Ferguson could go and chase herself for all she'd see of me.'

So this was the explanation of the woman's attitude, Jane was thinking. She felt free to criticise Aunt Ellen because she was not really paying her the wages she felt were her due. It was to Morris Leslie that this woman looked for supplementary payment, and the thought was disturbing.

The woman put her own thoughts into words as she said with a sour chuckle, 'Not that Ellen Ferguson would be grateful if she knew what he was doing! She's so proud she can't bear the thought of being beholden to him.'

While she spoke she was setting a tray and placing on it a dainty breakfast which was clearly for Aunt Ellen, and as Jane rose from her place at the table and strolled out into the grounds she had plenty to think about. It was clear that this Morris Leslie was a complex character. He had made it plain that he had no time for Aunt Ellen and yet he was keeping her in comfort in her old age by paying this woman to take care of her. It was also clear that this daily woman, in spite of her belligerent attitude, was an expert housekeeper: it was due to her energy that the house was so spotlessly clean and that Aunt Ellen was receiving the attention she needed in her old age. And it was thanks to Morris Leslie that this was so.

She walked slowly forward until she found a spot which had been a favourite of hers in childhood. It was a raised path which ran along what was almost a cliff top, so steeply did the ground fall away beneath it. From this high path there was a breathtaking view over the countryside, and Jane stopped and drew in her breath with annoyance as her eyes were drawn to that razed patch in the centre of the beautiful scene. Great trenches split the space which must have been several acres in extent; stumps of trees stood bare and white against the jagged soil.

Her aunt's horror of the destruction he had wrought was only too explicable when she gazed more closely at the scene before her. What kind of man could this Morris Leslie be to have brought such destruction to Windgates?

As she was gazing out, her anger rising with every minute, she heard the sound of a horse's hooves and turning, she found herself gazing up into the eyes of Morris Leslie who was riding slowly along the path behind her, on a magnificent sorrel.

He drew rein as he approached and for a moment sat still surveying the scene upon which she had been gazing. What was he thinking as he contemplated his handiwork? she wondered indignantly; but it was impossible to read his impassive face.

'And how did you find your aunt at the factor's house?' he asked after a moment or two.

'Oh!' Jane had not expected the question and was at a loss for an answer. But honesty compelled her to say slowly, 'I found her very comfortable. There have certainly been considerable changes made in the factor's house since I was last here. At first I didn't even recognise the spot. You've made the house very nice—rebuilt it, I'd say.'

He nodded. 'So I haven't exactly robbed your aunt, after all.'

34

'No,' Jane was forced to admit. 'I saw that she still has all her little treasures—the girandoles—I used to tinkle them when I was a child, and the music box that played Beethoven's Minuet, and—'

'And that hideously uncomfortable rosewood chair that has to be padded with cushions before one dare sit in it,' he added gravely. 'So you're satisfied with the situation you find your great-aunt in? You have no further complaints?'

'Not quite,' Jane told him stiffly.

'Oh? For instance?' he queried.

'For instance, just look at that!' Jane flung out her arm and pointed dramatically at the scene before them where the great gash he had created in the beauty of Windgates drew the eye. 'You're going to build hideous chalets there which will clash with the scenery and make an eyesore amongst what was once so lovely.'

For a moment he regarded her thoughtfully. 'People are more important than scenery,' he told her quietly. 'I'm going to give employment in Kirtleside, so that people will be able to stay here and earn their living.'

'Much you care about the poor people of Kirtleside!' cried Jane, indignantly. 'These chalets are to be for the rich so that they can come from all parts of the world and live in luxury and fish and shoot. A rich man's paradise, that's what you intend to make of Windgates.'

'You know, there is something to be said for the rich, Miss Talbot,' he told her very seriously. 'You see, we Leslies were hounded from our little croft and had to emigrate to Canada. Once there, we had to work like dogs for a bare living. If we prospered and grew rich—rich enough after a few generations for me to come back and buy the very land from which we were driven—that was because we never shirked hard work. If we became wealthy, we deserved to. And perhaps many of those who will come to fish and shoot here will have somewhat the same story. As for me, I'm in the habit of earning my living. What would become of me were I not to try to prosper and make money? No one would have pity on me now, no more than they had pity on those far-off Leslies who were left destitute when all they possessed was taken away from them.'

'But you're rich, you don't need to do this to Windgates,' she cried.

'And for how long would I be rich were I to be a fool and not make sure that the property I have bought becomes a paying concern?' he replied dryly.

'That's only an excuse to take your revenge on the Fergusons,' she cried. 'You don't need to do this to Windgates. You're doing it only because you're— you're a philistine and a vandal!'

He threw his head back and burst into laughter. 'Somehow that sounds familiar. If I'm not mistaken those are exactly the words Miss Ferguson used about me.'

He regarded her mockingly. 'By any chance are you aware, Miss Talbot, that when you get angry your eyes turn the most fascinating colour. I'm not a poet, but if I were I think I'd describe them as the colour of a still loch on a hot June day.'

Jane was so taken aback at this unexpected turn in the conversation that she felt the ground cut from beneath her. Then, as she realised that this had been his deliberate intention, she glared at him belligerently. He was trying to transform her anger into mere childish and ineffectual tantrums.

'I'm not interested in your opinion of my eyes,' she muttered sulkily.

To her dismay she realised that this retort did indeed sound extremely childish and inadequate. She ground her teeth impotently as once again he burst into laughter. If only she could think of something completely squashing to silence this dark mocking man, sitting with such an air of ease on his magnificent mount.

'You know, Miss Talbot, you're such a refreshing change from most of your sex. A compliment like that would have earned me a smile from any other girl, and you must admit it's not a bad effort from one who confesses he's no poet.'

'It's fairly obvious you're no poet,' Jane said acidly.

'Indeed! You interest me. Do you mean my appearance is not poetic enough—no thin ascetic features and tangled locks? No, I admit, as far as looks go, I wouldn't qualify.'

Jane tried to hold in her anger. He was openly making fun of her, she knew.

'No man with the smallest grain of sensibility could destroy Windgates as you are doing!'

'But I've already told you, my dear girl, that I'm giving local employment. Ask anyone in Kirtleside whether they'd clear off to Glasgow in preference to seeing a few trees razed to the ground and I think you'll find that, with the exception of a few fanatics, Kirtleside is solidly behind me.'

'In that case I number myself amongst the "few fanatics", as you call them,' Jane retorted.

Unknown to herself, in her anger she had approached close to him, and now with a sudden movement he bent down and, pulling her towards him, kissed her firmly on the lips.

Stunned by the suddenness and unexpectedness of this move, Jane had no time to resist, but pulled back with a gasp of alarm when he at last released her.

'That's for being such a beautiful little fanatic,' he said softly, then with a flip of the reins on the horse's neck, he rode off chuckling.

She had only herself to blame, Jane decided furiously as she watched him gallop towards the woods. By her very vehemence she had left herself open to his mockery, for she had no doubt that his kiss had been one of derision. After all, it was clear that Morris Leslie cared nothing at all about her opinion of him. She was only wasting her breath trying to reform a man who was obviously past such considerations. There was no hope for Aunt Ellen, she was reflecting glumly as she made her way back to the factor's house. It looked as if her aunt would just have to endure the agony of watching from her windows the transformation of the lands which had been in her family for generations.

At the factor's house she found Aunt Ellen in the sitting-room. 'Oh, there you are! And where have you been?' she snapped.

'Oh, I—I went out for a walk,' Jane told her. For an instant it had been on the tip of her tongue to tell her aunt of her encounter with Morris Leslie, but already she knew that any mention of him would be sure to enrage the old lady.

'Then you've missed breakfast,' Ellen told her. 'And what Maggie Crampsie will say about serving it to you at this hour of the day I don't know.'

'Oh, I've had breakfast,' Jane assured her. 'I was awake early and I went out for a walk.'

'If you've all that energy you can bring my summer coat down to Kirstag Bain and have her take it in for me for the hot weather,' Ellen told her. As she spoke she picked up a decidedly shabby pale blue linen coat which lay over the back of a chair and slipped it on. 'Fetch some pins from the work table,' she commanded.

As Jane regarded her aunt dressed in the shabby coat a lump came to her throat. It was obvious that it had seen wear during several summers. However, she did as she was bid and pinned it to suit her aunt's thinner figure.

As she was finishing, Maggie popped her head into the room. 'Well, I'm off now,' she informed Ellen. 'There's ham and salad in the fridge ready for lunch.' She paused for a moment regarding Jane on her knees placing the pins in place. 'Now why don't you get yourself a new coat, Miss Ferguson?' she said with a sort of gruff concern that warmed Jane's heart towards her. 'You've been wearing that old coat for the past three summers, if I'm not mistaken.'

'And where would I get the money for a new coat?' Ellen replied severely. 'Anyway, this is a fine piece of linen and it's almost impossible to wear out linen—which is just as well, as it will have to do me for another summer.'

Maggie Crampsie glanced at Jane and shook her head resignedly. 'Well, I'd better be off,' she said again cheerfully, and withdrew her head.

When the coat had been adjusted to Aunt Ellen's satisfaction, Jane packed it in a raffia shopping bag and strolled slowly down to the village. It was very much as she remembered it, although Kirstag Bain, the dressmaker, was a comparative newcomer, so Ellen had told her. She had come to Kirtleside from the Hebrides and was established in the last house in the village with her son, Dougal, who at one time had been employed by Morris Leslie but who had injured himself during some tree felling.

At the last house in the village, which turned out to be a small two-storied building of granite blocks, Jane knocked for some time. The door was slightly ajar and she could hear a faint whirring and the sound of humming, but no one came to open it to her. Eventually she gently pushed the door and found herself looking across a narrow hallway into a small back room in which sat a short, round energetic-looking woman who was running a seemingly endless length of fabric through an electric sewing machine and humming to herself while she did so.

She looked up, caught Jane's eye and waved her in as she went on with hemming the material. 'There, that's the last of those curtains,' she said with a sigh of relief as she drew the material out of the machine at last and snipped a thread. 'Two or three hundred miles of hemming at the very least! And now what can I do for you?' As she spoke she swept a bundle of cuttings off a chair and indicated that Jane should be seated.

As Jane drew out the linen coat from the raffia shopping bag Kirstag said, 'Dear me, don't I know that coat! It's Miss Ferguson's, isn't it, and don't tell me she wants it altered again.'

'Yes, it's to be taken in,' Jane told her. 'I've marked it with pins.'

The dressmaker turned the coat in her hands. 'So it has to be taken in again! Dear me, Miss Ferguson has got very thin—but it's not to be wondered at. She has had a lot of trouble and worry in the past few years.

Although I must say she does take things very much to heart.'

This was obviously the dressmaker's mild way of saying that Ellen was a woman who found it almost impossible to reconcile herself to the change in her circumstances, and Jane, glancing around the dull shadowed little room with its floor scattered with cuttings and scraps of thread, could not but compare her aunt's lot with that of this little woman who somehow seemed to be able to keep cheerful in the face of adversity.

'However, no doubt Miss Ferguson will feel ever so much better now that you've come to keep her company,' the dressmaker continued. 'You're her great-niece, aren't you?'

'And how did you know that?' Jane asked.

Kirstag gave a merry bubbling laugh. 'My dear, it was all over the village in about a half an hour after you had arrived. Believe me, news travels fast in these little places. We've nothing else to do but gossip about our neighbours.'

'My aunt is very unhappy about what is being done at Windgates and I don't know if my being here will be of much help to her,' Jane said doubtfully.

The dressmaker made a great business of folding up the long curtains upon which she had been at work. 'One can see your aunt's point of view, of course,' she conceded in a curiously muffled tone of voice, her back turned to Jane, 'and indeed there's no doubt about it that Mr Leslie can be a difficult man to get on with. But at the same time he does give employment, and that's important to the likes of people like me who have to live on very little.'

Slowly she wrapped the curtains in a big sheet of

brown paper and tied it with string as she went on, her head lowered, 'You see, my son Dougal used to work for him, and I must say he gave a very fair wage—which is more than some do around here where they know work is so hard to come by. If Dougal's out of work now he has only himself to blame. I don't try to put it off on Mr Leslie. Dougal, you see, was employed at the timber felling and a nice little wage he was bringing in. You can imagine how welcome it was, for it's hard to keep two people on what a dressmaker earns. But now he's laid up. You see, he disobeyed orders and a branch fell on his foot. He's getting better and the doctor says he'll be as good as new any day now. But Mr Leslie says he'll never employ him again. Oh, he paid compensation while Dougal was laid up, but now that he's getting better that will stop and what we're to do I really don't know.'

Jane looked into the troubled face which the little dressmaker raised to hers. She looked around the dim poverty-stricken little room and her indignation against Morris Leslie grew. 'But why won't he take your son back?' she asked abruptly.

'Oh, he's a hard man, no doubt,' Kirstag said miserably, 'but on the other hand Dougal can be forgetful at times—as I've very good reason to know myself. Send him on an errand and he'll come back and tell you that he's forgotten what you asked him to do. Dougal's injury was his own fault. If he had obeyed orders he wouldn't have been hurt, and that's the sort of thing Mr Leslie can't forgive.'

She eyed Jane doubtfully for a moment, then said in an altered tone of voice, 'I suppose you think it strange I'm telling you all this, but I was wondering if you would just ask him as a special favour to take Dougal back into his employment. I'm sure he has learned his lesson and, if Mr Leslie wants it, I'll have Dougal apologise properly for the trouble he has caused.'

Jane shook her head slowly as her mind went back to her interview with Morris Leslie early that morning when he had come riding along the cliff path on his sorrel horse. She had lashed out at him then—something Morris Leslie was not likely to forget if he was as merciless as all those connected with him seemed to believe.

'I'm afraid I'd have no influence with him, Mrs Bain,' she told the little dressmaker. 'As a matter of fact I'm already in his black books myself. You see, my aunt feels—' she hesitated, wondering how to put into words the antagonism that existed between Ellen Ferguson and the new owner of Windgates.

'Your aunt naturally feels bad at losing her old home,' Kirstag said, 'but on the other hand he has built a lovely wee house for her, whereas I am—well, you can see for yourself.' With a wave of her hand she indicated the dingy room and Jane had a guilty feeling that Ellen Ferguson was needlessly bemoaning her fate, which was certainly lighter than that of this little woman.

'Och, I see how it is,' Kirstag went on with an effort to speak cheerfully. 'Miss Ferguson is at daggers drawn with Mr Leslie, and naturally, being her great-niece, you take her part.'

Yes, it was something like that, Jane was thinking. No need to tell the little dressmaker that, combined with her natural championing of her aunt's cause, she had also conceived an instant dislike for the arrogant man who had taken the house that had once been Ellen

43

Ferguson's!

'Could you call for the coat in about a week?' Kirstag said, changing the subject. 'I'd get down to it sooner, but I've a wedding dress to do this week. But I'll hurry it along as well as I can.'

'Yes, I'll come back in about a week to pick up the coat,' Jane told Kirstag as she went out.

As she strolled along the village street she was overtaken by a small blue car and as it drew to a stop she recognised Gregory Shields' red head.

'Hello,' he leaned out. 'I'm in luck meeting you again. If you're not in a hurry could you have elevenses with me?'

Jane looked at his narrow, eager, freckled face regarding her from the rather battered blue car and nodded. 'Yes, I'd like that.' She felt a short while in Gregory's company would wash away the disturbing events of the morning: her angry interview with Morris Leslie and the equally distressing story told her by Kirstag concerning Morris's treatment of her son.

'Remain where you are for just a moment, while I park the limousine, and I'll be with you,' he told her cheerfully.

Swiftly he turned the little car into a side lane that led off the main village street, jumped out and joined her, and together they strolled along the street until the young doctor stopped outside one of the terraced granite block houses and rapped on the door with the brass knocker made in the form of a hand.

The door was opened by a short stout lady wearing an apron, her hands floury.

'Any chance of coffee and a hot honey bun, Miss MacKillop?' he asked ingratiatingly.

'This is my baking morning, Dr Shields—as well

you know,' Miss MacKillop told him with mock severity. 'And I'm up to my eyebrows in work.'

'So I can see,' he returned, as she drew her arm across her forehead leaving a smear of white flour across one brow.

'Och well, come away in,' she said with mock resignation, 'and I'll see what I can do. But I do declare you're able to smell the baking a mile off, you're always so sure to turn up just as a batch of buns is due out of the oven.'

She ushered them into a small parlour, the floor covered with linoleum, and there they established themselves at a small round table covered with a felt cloth edged with bobbles.

While they waited Jane had time to observe that on the shelved mantelpiece were many portraits in silver frames, several of them of the same young man in military uniform.

'I may as well tell you that when I come here alone I am admitted to the kitchen,' he told Jane, sotto voce. 'We're being relegated to this cold parlour because you're still a stranger. But some day, if all goes well, you'll become one of the community and you'll be able to eat your honey bun in the warmth of the kitchen.'

'I do hope that some day I may qualify,' Jane told him equally sotto voce, for in spite of the warm weather there was a distinct chill in the air of the parlour. Miss MacKillop couldn't come soon enough with the warming coffee, she was thinking.

'The portraits are of Miss MacKillop's young man who was killed in action,' Gregory told her. 'She has certainly been true to his memory. And now tell me how you're settling down at your aunt's home.'

'You didn't tell me what had happened,' Jane told

him a little resentfully.

'No, I wanted you to find out for yourself—and I can see from your expression that you have. Well, what do you think of the situation?'

'I don't know what to think,' Jane said slowly. 'At first, I admit, I was very upset when I heard that my aunt was staying at what we used to call "the factor's house" because when I was here last it was hardly more than a ruin. But now—'

'Now you see it done up—rebuilt, actually, you're quite reconciled,' he rejoined dryly.

'Well, there's no doubt that my aunt is comfortable. She has a nice home there and somehow she has been able to keep all her old pieces of furniture and ornaments which she treasured so much,' Jane said slowly, trying hard to be fair.

'And yet your aunt is not happy,' he told her.

'Yes, that's so,' Jane admitted. 'She hates to see that dreadful gash in the valley where Morris Leslie has cut down such a great extent of trees. Aunt Ellen dreads the thought of the valley being filled with horrible modern chalets, quite out of keeping with the scene.'

'And how do you feel about all this?' he asked after a moment.

'I hate it,' she said passionately, then fell silent as Miss MacKillop returned bearing a laden tray.

'I was glad to hear you say that, Jane,' he told her when Miss MacKillop had departed. 'I admit I can't stand the man. He's ruining Kirtleside. Oh, I'm not so old-fashioned that I don't want improvements—but not as he is setting about it. I'm not an ambitious man, Jane. All I ever wanted out of life was to be a doctor here in Kirtleside as my father had been before me. Morris Leslie is inclined to sneer at me and to pretend that I'm an old fuddy-duddy who's totally averse to improvements. Far from it. Nobody wants prosperity for the district more than I do. I want the people here to be happy, and in my own small way—in services to the community—I may say that I've contributed something. All I ask is that prosperity should not come to Kirtleside in such a guise that the countryside is going to be changed so radically that we're not going to recognise it as the same place. Oh, Morris Leslie makes great play of the benefits he's bringing to the place, but in my eyes he's nothing more than a vandal.'

Jane nodded. This was exactly her attitude.

'There's another point about his rebuilding the factor's house and establishing Miss Ferguson there, and that is that there was something ugly about his coming from Canada and buying the home of the very people who were the cause of his family being forced to emigrate. The Fergusons had owned that land for hundreds of years. Ellen Ferguson was the last of her line and it looked bad to people here that a Leslie should return and crow over her—the last representative of the family who had wronged his, as he thought. It's my belief that he gave her " the factor's house " just to appease local feeling. While she's there no one can say that he has treated the old family too badly or taken too crude a revenge. But that is exactly what he's doing. It's a refinement of torture for her to be forced to look out from her window and see the upheaval he's creating in the lands that once were hers. But then you're not exactly smitten dumb with admiration of Morris Leslie.'

'I hate him,' she told him, her eyes flashing.

'Let's shake hands on our mutual hatred, then,' he told her with a grin, 'for that's exactly how I feel towards him too.'

It was at this point, just as they were solemnly shaking hands, that Miss MacKillop opened the door and thrust her head into the room. 'Well, and how did you like the honey buns?' she inquired of Jane.

'They were simply delicious,' Jane told her. 'Far too tasty. I've eaten too many.'

'Oh, well, you mustn't be worrying about your figure at your age,' Miss MacKillop informed her. 'Not that you'd need to—slim as a wand as you are. What about me—but then I never worry about such things.'

'And it shows up in your honey buns,' Gregory told her, solemnly. 'They spread happiness wherever they're found.'

'Now go on with your flattery,' Miss MacKillop enjoined. 'But seriously,' turning to Jane, 'you must call in one of these evenings and I promise you a treat. You know, we Scots learned the art of pastry cooking from the French in the time of Mary Queen of Scots, and I pride myself that my pastries are every bit as good as the French any day.'

'You must give me your solemn promise never to eat as much as one of Miss MacKillop's cream cakes,' Gregory cried in mock alarm. 'No figure on earth, however slim, is proof against them. And as for eating only one! Once started it's impossible to stop again. Promise, won't you?'

'Now, enough of that,' Miss MacKillop admonished. 'My cream cakes are as light as air, as well you know. They wouldn't as much as put an ounce on anyone.'

Having received Jane's promise to call some evening and, completely free of charge, consume as many cream

48

cakes as her heart desired, Miss MacKillop bade them a cheery goodbye and then went out, the young doctor driving Jane back to the entrance to Windgates. As she was about to turn away with a parting wave of her hand, he leaned out of the window to inquire, 'By the way, just how good are you at Scottish dancing?'

'Not good at all,' Jane informed him. 'In fact I know nothing whatsoever about it.'

'Then in that case I must give you a few lessons. It wouldn't do if you were to disgrace me at the forthcoming ceilidh.'

He paused, and Jane was keenly aware that he was awaiting her answer with interest. Did she really want to become involved with this young man? she asked herself. Not yet, she knew, and without committing herself to accepting the implied invitation she turned away with a laugh and a wave of her hand. She could hear Gregory's car move off along the road, then as she turned her head she found herself gazing straight into the eyes of Morris Leslie, whose car was edging towards the gates.

'Well, it certainly didn't take you long to become acclimatised,' he said coldly. 'Already, no doubt, you've had the opportunity to learn the attitude of the village doctor towards me. I suppose he has been filling your ear with his views on the vandal who come from abroad to wreck Kirtleside. And when he's not at hand there's your aunt dropping poison into your ear against me.'

This was all so true that for a moment Jane was silent. 'I don't suppose my opinion can be of much interest to you,' she countered stiffly.

'On the contrary, I care a great deal,' he told her, a wry smile altering his expression, and she was disturbedly aware of how attractive this man could be when he chose.

'But why should you?' she said awkwardly. 'I'm a newcomer here; my opinion can hardly have much weight with you.'

'You underestimate yourself. Has it not occurred to you that men are prone to be susceptible to pretty young women?'

Was he once again mocking her? she wondered. Would it not be judicious to beat a hasty retreat before she became an object of further derision? Yet, in spite of herself, she said impulsively, 'You seem to be the type of man who doesn't care a jot what anyone thinks of him.'

'Then you're wrong. I'm as susceptible as most men to a pretty face. Remember that, Jane.'

She had a glimpse of white teeth against tanned skin. Then the car raced off through the gates.

So he had, for the first time, called her Jane! As she continued along the avenue she found herself curiously disturbed by that short encounter with Morris Leslie. How like him to challenge her crudely about whether Gregory had been discussing him with her! It was the sort of harsh, uncompromising attack that she knew was typical of the man: he had nothing but contempt for the refinements of civilised society.

A vandal in every sense of the word, she was thinking angrily as she turned off along the broad driveway that led towards Aunt Ellen's house. But he had also, she recognised, a dangerous charm.

CHAPTER III

It was some days later and Jane was idly swinging in a hammock in the garden surrounding Aunt Ellen's house, reading a paperback and munching an apple. Amongst the surrounding trees the birds sang sweetly and the scent of lilac from a dark purple bush nearby was carried to her in little waves as the soft breeze blew in her direction. Jane was feeling at her most con-She raised her head and could see her aunt outlined tented when she heard Ellen's voice calling her. in the window of the sitting-room. 'Could you come in for a moment, Jane?'

Jane put down her paperback and flung her apple core into the corner of the garden where after a moment's eyeing it shrewdly a bird hopped down to peck at it.

In the sitting-room she found Ellen seated at her writing-bureau.

She scribbled a cheque and thrust it angrily into an envelope. 'And there's that philistine's rent for the month!' she exclaimed. 'I wonder if it would be too much trouble, Jane, for you to deliver this to the house. I'm a day or two behind, and I wouldn't for the world have that man be able to say that I don't pay my rent on the dot.'

Instantly Jane agreed, although as a rule she made a point of keeping as far away from the main house as possible. But any service she could do Aunt Ellen was a pleasure for her. For an instant she hesitated, debating with herself whether she would go to her roo mand tidy herself up before making the short journey, then decided that it wasn't really necessary. It was hardly likely that Morris Leslie would be about at that time in the afternoon. He was nearly always out of the house attending to the multitude of decisions that had to be made in connection with the vast transaction that was involved in transforming Windgates into a paying concern. So it didn't matter that she was wearing a very simple cotton dress, rather rumpled from lying in the hammock, that her hair was distinctly less than tidy, and that her bare legs showed scratches from gooseberry picking. She would simply pop the envelope through the letter box and hurry back to the sanctuary of the factor's house as soon as possible.

But as she was moving away, Ellen put paid to this resolve. Her figure again appeared silhouetted in the sitting-room window and she called out, 'And be sure to get a receipt! Give it to Mr Ogre himself and to no one else. I don't want him to be able to say that he didn't get it.'

'Oh, do you think he'll be there?' Jane asked, a little dismayed.

'Well, if he isn't, bring it back and you can take it another time when he's in,' Aunt Ellen replied inexorably.

For a moment Jane hovered irresolutely. If Morris Leslie were to be at Windgates and if she must place the rent in his hands and no others, then perhaps she really should make some effort to tidy herself. Then she tilted her head defiantly. What did she care what Morris Leslie thought of her? She didn't give one snap of her fingers how she appeared in his eyes, she told herself with a decisiveness to match Aunt Ellen's, and, with this thought, she turned off along the path towards the main house.

She was about to knock on the main door when it opened and Mrs McInnes appeared on the scene. She was dressed to go out, but hailed Jane affably. 'Well now, come away in,' she exclaimed. 'Were you just about to call on Mr Leslie?'

'I'm bringing the rent for my aunt,' Jane told her.

'Oh well, in that case perhaps you'd better see the new secretary,' the housekeeper told her with a curious air of withdrawal.

'Oh.' Jane looked her surprise at the news as she stepped into the hall through the door which the housekeeper held invitingly open.

'Yes, we have a new secretary,' Mrs McInnes told her tightly as she led the way across the hall, 'and between you and me she's a pretty lofty lady. Oh yes, she has arrived and has taken over the library—and pretty nearly everything else here, I may tell you. She even tried to interfere with *me*,' the housekeeper added with emphasis, 'but I know my rights and I drew the line. No one steps into my province, or only over my dead body, I told her, and I must say that made her ladyship think.'

As she spoke she rapped none too gently upon the library door and when a voice inside called, 'Come in,' she ushered Jane into the room and made her departure, and Jane found herself staring across the room at the woman who now sat behind the big table in the place where Morris Leslie had once 'interviewed' her for the job now held by this newcomer.

The new secretary fixed her with an inquiring eye. 'Well, anything I can do for you?' she asked.

Jane had a first impression of a slender perfectly groomed woman with a mass of striking tawny hair combed high into a chignon. She was dressed in dark blue with touches of white and against her shoulder sparkled a small but evidently costly piece of jewellery.

' I've—I've come to pay the rent,' Jane began, feeling curiously ill at ease in the presence of this self-possessed woman.

' In that case come in, won't you: don't just hover at the door.'

In silent mortification Jane stepped into the room and closed the door behind her.

' Well, give it to me.' The woman held out her hand and reluctantly Jane approached the table. ' You live in one of the cottages in the village, I suppose,' the secretary said pleasantly.

' No, this is Miss Ferguson's rent,' Jane told her.

Now that she had approached nearer she saw that she was decidedly older than herself: beautifully made-up with fine pale skin and an air of poise and sophistication that instantly stamped her as being perfectly efficient. Into Jane's mind came snatches of that letter Morris Leslie had read out on that first evening when he had supposed she herself had been applying for the position now held by this tawny-headed woman. This would be Rhoda Mannering, Jane realised, the girl who had applied stating that she had held a position of trust and responsibility with satisfaction for several years and who desired a job in the country because she was interested in country pursuits. She would ride and swim, Jane immediately decided, picturing that slender taut figure in riding clothes or swim suit.

' Miss Ferguson? I'm afraid I don't quite know who that is. I'm Rhoda Mannering, Mr Leslie's secretary. I've not been here very long, so I haven't caught up with who is who yet. However, I'm learning.' She smiled pleasantly at Jane and again held out her hand for the envelope.

'I'm afraid my aunt instructed me to give this only to Mr Leslie,' Jane said almost apologetically. It must sound ludicrous to Rhoda Mannering, she guessed—but then this newcomer could know nothing of the peculiar circumstances surrounding Ellen Ferguson's becoming tenant of the factor's house and her feud with the new owner of Windgates.

Rhoda Mannering eyed her thoughtfully for a moment. 'I'll give you a receipt, of course, if that's the problem,' she said tentatively.

'I'm afraid that won't do,' Jane said, growing even more embarrassed. 'My aunt said the rent was to be given into Mr Leslie's hands.'

'But this is ridiculous,' the secretary exclaimed. 'In future all such matters will be handled by me, so we may as well set off on the right foot. Anyway, I couldn't possibly interrupt Mr Leslie about such a trivial affair.'

'Then he is here at Windgates at the moment?' Jane said.

'Yes, he's here,' Rhoda admitted. 'But as I said, I couldn't possibly interrupt him about anything so unimportant.'

'Then I'm afraid I'll have to take the rent back to my aunt,' Jane told her lamely, feeling acutely the ridiculous position she was in. 'However, since he's here just now, I don't see why I shouldn't deliver it into his hands. I won't detain him a moment. I'm sure he won't mind.'

Again Rhoda Mannering eyed her thoughtfully. 'You told me you're not paying the rent for one of the cottages in the village,' she said slowly. 'Just who are you, then?'

'My aunt's Miss Ferguson,' Jane told her. 'She has the tenancy of the factor's house—it's in the grounds,' she added helpfully, seeing that Rhoda still fixed her with an inquiring gaze.

'Mr Leslie has given her a house in the grounds,' Rhoda repeated thoughtfully. 'She's a retired member of his staff, perhaps?'

'Not quite,' Jane said dryly. 'She is the former owner of Windgates.'

'Oh well, I suppose—in that case—' the secretary said reluctantly, and pressed a button on the intercom on her table. 'Could you come to the library for a moment, Mr Leslie?'

She clicked off the connection and they waited in a strained silence until the door was thrown open and Morris Leslie strode into the room with that curious air of leashed energy that characterised him.

A grin crossed his face as his eyes fell on Jane. 'Oh, it's you, is it?' he greeted her. 'I'm amazed you have nerve enough to venture into the lair of the philistine. Surely you're taking your life in your hands.'

His manner was easy and bantering and Jane was aware that in Rhoda Mannering's gaze as she looked quickly from one to the other there was a certain amount of surprise. Evidently she had expected him to be irritated by this incursion into his time. And she had a momentary sense of elation which she instantly stifled at the thought that her stock had immediately risen in Miss Mannering's estimation.

'And what can I do for you?'

'It's just my aunt's rent,' Jane began, 'she—'

'She said you were to be sure that it was delivered straight into my hands, isn't that it?' he asked, in his manner a distinct contemptuousness that made her hackles rise and overcame the momentary pleasure she had felt in his first easy greeting.

'Yes, I told her I could deal with such a trivial matter,' Rhoda Mannering had instantly divined his change of mood. 'But she insisted on seeing you.'

'Very well, give it to me,' he told Jane with an air of irritated weariness. He held out his hand. She placed the envelope in it and he tossed it on to the secretary's table. 'Give her a receipt for it, Rhoda,' he instructed abruptly.

As she drew a receipt pad towards her and began to enter the particulars, he turned to Jane with an air of irritation. 'Why must we have this tiresome charade month after month?' he demanded.

But Jane's eyes were on that envelope tossed so carelessly on the secretary's table. That rent for the factor's house, which to him was so trivial, meant quite a lot to Aunt Ellen. She was not well off. She had to live, Jane had discovered, on the interest coming to her from the investment of the money he had paid her for Windgates—not so very much considering the profit he would probably win from the property once it was put on a paying basis. This rent was an important item in Aunt Ellen's budget. And once again she felt her anger rising up against this man to whom other people's lives meant so little. 'I'm sure I don't know,' she replied tartly. 'I'm just a messenger, remember. This has nothing to do with me.'

He said nothing for a moment, but Jane, without glancing at him, was aware of his amusement.

'Ah well, if this is a tactless subject—and what else can one expect from a philistine and a vandal—perhaps we could talk about something else. Tell me,

Miss Talbot, how are you enjoying your stay at Kirtleside? How does life in the Highlands compare with London?'

As Jane did not reply, because she felt almost too angry to speak, Rhoda Mannering joined in with a sort of obvious tact that Jane found irritating, ' Oh, you've lived in London, have you? You don't belong to the Highlands, then!'

' No, I came here only recently,' Jane replied, glad of the opportunity of turning her attention away from Morris Leslie. ' I've lived all my life in London. Apart from a short holiday here when I was a child, I've never visited Scotland before.'

' Really, this is interesting,' Rhoda said with artificial attention. ' And what did you do in London?'

' I was an audio-typist,' Jane told her stiffly. ' But only in a typing pool, of course.'

A faint smile crossed Rhoda Mannering's lips. ' Oh yes, I know the sort of thing. I did my share of typing. But I confess I found it boring. I prefer responsibility. I like the excitement of working in partnership with a man who is going places and doing big things in an interesting way.' Here her glance flitted momentarily to Morris Leslie.

' You'll find plenty of excitement here at Kirtleside,' Morris Leslie told her ironically. ' I believe the next great event of interest is the ceilidh.' His eyes were on Jane as he spoke. ' Tell me, are you going to patronise it?'

' I have been invited,' she told him coldly.

' I needn't ask by whom,' he rejoined. ' Our local doctor is a persistent advocate of native interests. He's a great believer in the past—a past that so many people have cause to remember to their sorrow.'

'Then it's true that "our local doctor" and I have something in common,' Jane told him angrily. 'For I too believe in the Kirtleside of long ago. It was a wonderful place to live in. There was plenty of good here as well as evil. I think it just depends upon what sort of person you are, if you aren't able to make something of your life in an old-fashioned place without having to root it up and change everything to suit oneself. It seems to me that you're just filled with bitterness and hatred and—and—'

As she drew to a halt, biting her lip to prevent herself saying something really unforgivable, Rhoda Mannering broke in again with her obvious and irritating tact, 'This ceilidh, just what is it? It sounds so interesting.'

'It's a sort of social evening, Rhoda,' Morris Leslie told her. 'With singing and dancing, sometimes pipe playing and so on: local talent is called on and a good time is had by one and all.'

'But that sounds fascinating,' the secretary exclaimed. 'I've travelled quite a lot and have seen many parts of the world, and I always find it very educative to absorb as much local colour as possible wherever I go. I have recordings of Neapolitan songs, and flamenco music from Spain. I suppose they sing songs in the native language?' she turned to her employer.

'I must admit I haven't attended any such gatherings since I arrived,' he told her, 'but yes, it seems that they sing songs both in Gaelic and in English. Miss Talbot should find it interesting—that is, if you can stand the pipes,' he remarked, his attention again returning to Jane.

'I must say I found the Greek pipes fascinating,'

Rhoda Mannering told him. 'I remember one evening at a night-club in Athens one of the turns was some native dancing and singing: the performers wore Greek national dress, and I found it perfectly thrilling.'

As she spoke she tore the receipt from the pad and held it out towards Jane, but Morris Leslie took it from her fingers and moved with Jane towards the door.

'You know, it's rather a pity you're bespoke for the ceilidh,' he told her with mock earnestness as they walked across the hall.

'And why is that?' she asked warily.

'Because I might have summoned up enough courage to ask you if you would come with me,' he told her.

Jane gave a little gasp of annoyance. 'I'm perfectly sure you would have found such a simple, unsophisticated entertainment insufferably boring,' she told him acidly, holding her hand out for the receipt.

'Are you always such a little spitfire, or is it simply that I bring the worst out in you?' he asked as he slowly placed the slip of paper in her fingers.

Abruptly she took her departure, but as she went off around the side of the house she glanced back to find him standing on the doorstep watching her departure. He gave a sardonic wave of the hand before turning back into the house.

That evening Jane began to look through her wardrobe with a critical eye to the dress she would wear at the ceilidh. One by one she took out her dresses and laid them on her bed. The door was ajar and suddenly she became aware of Ellen Ferguson standing regarding her curiously. 'What on earth are you doing, child?'

'Oh, I'm looking out a dress for the ceilidh,' Jane

told her cheerfully. A little ruefully she surveyed the garments on the bed: none of them seemed to be quite right for the occasion and suddenly she realised that it was quite some time since she had had anything new. Her stepmother had seen to it that her allowance from her father had been cut to the minimum and to please his new wife Jane's father had reluctantly agreed to reduce the small sum he had been in the habit of giving his daughter for clothes. It had all been part of the undying dislike his new wife had conceived for her stepdaughter: she had bitterly resented the smallest attention he had paid to Jane, jealously hoarding his every word and look for herself. It had only been one more tiny straw in the wind to show that inevitably they must part.

Ellen Ferguson's verdict on Jane's wardrobe bore out her own attitude. 'There's nothing here that I'd care to see you turn up in,' she told Jane with characteristic bluntness. 'You must have a new dress. We'll buy some material and have Kirstag Bain run it up for you.'

'Oh no, Aunt Ellen, I wouldn't think of such a thing!' Jane protested.

As the days had passed she had come to realise how frugally Ellen lived: every penny was hoarded and spent to the best advantage. And now Jane, glancing at Ellen's own clothes, was keenly aware of how old-fashioned and shabby they were.

When she tried to hint something of this her aunt brushed the objection aside. 'Nonsense, child, what does it matter what I wear? At my age no one expects me to be a fashion-plate. I feel far more comfortable and at home in my old, well-worn tweeds and tartans. Anyway, that's the best of Scottish cloths, you simply can't wear them out, and I cannot bring myself to part with them. But with you it's a different matter: you must turn up at this ceilidh looking your best and do me credit.'

Jane protested stoutly, but when her aunt clinched the argument with the plea that by appearing in an old dress she would be letting down the Fergusons, she finally gave in with a sigh.

'Anyway, it needn't cost the earth,' Ellen concluded. 'It's not done to turn up in anything too elaborate. Something simple and pretty is quite enough. Buy some inexpensive material and Kirstag will charge very little to run it up for you.'

So it was that early next morning Jane found herself on the bus which ran through the village four times a week on her way to Aberdeen to buy dress material. She enjoyed the trip: the countryside was at its most beautiful: the distant soft misty blues and mauves of the mountains were restful to the eyes: a little breeze rippled the waters of a loch and turned the surface into a sea of miniature waves.

As they drove into the granite city she found that she was quite looking forward to selecting a dress length of material in spite of the fact that the sum of money Aunt Ellen had pressed into her hand had seemed to her quite inadequate. But the thought of the generosity of that gift brought a lump to her throat. In her rough, gruff way Aunt Ellen was turning out a brick, and with every day that passed Jane felt more fond of the old lady with her sometimes cantankerous ways.

With every day that passed too her resentment against Morris Leslie seemed to grow. Not that she would allow herself to think of him, she told herself: this morning she would just enjoy herself. She stopped off for tea and cake at one of the attractive restaurants in Union Street, then crossed the street and went into one of the big stores, its floors softly carpeted, where were displayed exquisite clothes, fabrics and perfumes from all parts of the world.

In the fabric department she permitted herself an enjoyable look around regardless of price, before she would settle to the serious business of getting something as attractive as possible within her price range. Very shortly her eye fell upon a beautiful material patterned in gold and orange. Eagerly she fingered the cloth which would, she knew, drape wonderfully.

'Why don't you take a look at it in one of the mirrors?' the assistant suggested.

'Oh, it's far too dear,' Jane said hurriedly. 'I'm looking for something quite simple and inexpensive. I was just admiring it.'

'Why not see how it looks, at any rate?' urged the assistant.

He took up the heavy bolt of cloth and they moved across to where a long mirror swung on a frame. Here in a good light Jane was able to drape the material across her shoulders and see how wonderfully the glowing colour seemed to enhance the nutty brown of her curls. As she had expected, it draped wonderfully. For a moment she stood regarding it wistfully, then as she was about to take it from her shoulders a voice behind her said, 'Certainly the ideal thing for you. Have you decided on it?' And with a little gasp she found that she was gazing into the eyes of Morris Leslie in the mirror.

She swung around abruptly, almost entangling herself in the length of material.

'What—what are you doing here?' she asked, disconcerted.

'Just strolling around,' he told her with a grin. 'I've been purchasing a few handkerchiefs. Any objection? But you haven't answered my question. Do you intend to purchase this fabric?'

'Certainly not,' Jane replied, disentangling herself from the length of cloth.

'And why not, may I ask? It certainly suits you.'

'Because it's too dear, that's why,' Jane told him crossly. 'Aunt Ellen couldn't possibly afford to buy me a dress of such expensive stuff. After all, I'm not going to a ball.'

'What Aunt Ellen doesn't know will do her no harm,' he pronounced. He nodded to the assistant. 'Let's have a dress length of this stuff for the young lady.'

'How dare you!' gasped Jane. 'I won't take it.'

'Not even if I insist?'

'Certainly not. Especially not if you insist.'

'Then I must find some other use for it: I might perhaps have it made up into curtains—for the kitchen,' he ended thoughtfully.

'Oh, you're—you're—'

'A philistine and a vandal,' he reminded her.

By this time the material had been neatly parcelled. Morris Leslie paid the amount and seizing the parcel caught Jane by the elbow. The whole transaction had been carried out so swiftly that she found herself being propelled from the shop still protesting.

A short distance away was his car. He opened the door and tossed the parcel into the back seat. 'Now perhaps we should have tea,' he said thoughtfully, studying Jane's furious face.

'I've already had tea,' she retorted.

'Then we can set off for Kirtleside immediately,' he told her. 'Get in.'

'I wouldn't dream of it,' Jane told him angrily. 'I came by bus and I'll go back by bus. Besides, I haven't bought my material yet and—'

'Enough of this nonsense!' he interrupted. He flung open the door and somehow Jane found herself seated in the front of the car and he was taking his place beside her at the wheel. In a very few minutes they were driving past the handsome granite houses of the suburbs and into the country.

'Did I hear you say you weren't going to a ball?' he broke the sulky silence in which Jane had wrapped herself. 'Surely I must have misheard. You probably said you *were* going to a ball.'

'Certainly not,' she answered. 'And that's just what's so stupid about buying such expensive cloth. I was just looking at it—admiring it. I was going to buy something quite simple for the ceilidh.'

'Oh, so that's when it's going to be worn! But you'll look perfectly stunning in a dress of orange and gold at the ceilidh.'

'I should look no such thing,' she told him angrily. 'I should just look stupid. Everyone wears simple inexpensive dresses at these affairs, and—'

'Tell me,' he interrupted, 'do you know how to do Scottish dancing? Will you be able to join in?'

'No, I won't be able to,' she admitted. 'I don't know the steps.'

'Then you must permit me to give you a few lessons.'

'You?' she exclaimed in surprise.

'Oh yes, there are sides to my character which you haven't dreamed of,' he told her solemnly. 'You see, we exiles in Canada kept up with the things of the homeland. Scottish dancing is very popular and every year we have meetings at which the pipes are played and there are competitions for Scottish music and dancing. When singers or dancers come from the homelands we have to hire the largest arenas in the district to accommodate all who wish to attend.'

'Oh!' was all Jane could say. This was something she had not dreamed of and she found herself glancing momentarily at this strange dynamic man who could be so unexpected and disconcerting.

'Yes, when I was a child I was taught Scottish dancing,' he said. 'I've always kept up my interest in Scottish music, and I even know a few words of the Gaelic.'

Jane was silent, feeling curiously disturbed by what he had told her. Her attitude towards him was softened and she was about to question him about his life in Canada when a vivid picture flashed before her mind of the expression on his face when he had flung down the envelope containing Ellen's rent money on the table before his secretary.

'I'm surprised to hear that you take an interest in these old-world things,' she said coldly. 'It seems strange to hear it from a man like you, who looks only to the future.'

'Is that true, I wonder,' he said musingly. 'That I look only to the future? You know, there's a certain amount of truth in some of your aunt's complaints about me. She doesn't understand my motives, of course, but it's true that I came back out of nostalgia. It just happened that Windgates was for sale when I returned to Kirtleside and as soon as I saw it I wanted it and knew that somehow I must have it. It's true to say that no matter how go-ahead a man may be, still for those whose people have been exiles there's always a certain amount of looking back towards the homeland. As the song has it,

" Though mists divide us and a waste of seas,
    Yet still the heart is Highland
    And we in dreams behold the Hebrides." '

Jane, listening, found tears come to her eyes, and suddenly she realised how musical his voice was.

As he said the words they were turning in through the wide entrance of Windgates. Swiftly he drove along the avenue and turned off along the broad path which now led to the factor's house.

Abruptly Jane sat up. ' Oh, don't! ' she exclaimed.

Instantly his expression altered. ' Don't drive you home, you mean?' he asked coldly.

Jane was silent. She could not admit to him the fantastic lengths to which Ellen Ferguson carried her hatred of the man whom she believed was plundering her ancestral home.

' I'd—I'd rather you didn't drive me right to the door,' she said in a low tone.

' Because you're afraid of your aunt's disapproval,' he told her, contempt in his voice.

As she did not reply, he went on, ' Your aunt will have to accept the truth that I am the new owner of Windgates and become used to the idea.'

Jane could feel herself stiffen. Bitterly she blamed herself for allowing herself to become softened by his conversation during the drive home. She might have known that under that momentary sentimentality there was still the same granite-hard man she had such good cause to dislike.

As the car stopped before the expanse of lawn that

separated the factor's house from the drive she sprang out. 'You're horrible, horrible!' she blazed. 'You think of nothing but power and money, and—'

'And I don't care a fig what you think of me,' he returned with an anger that matched her own.

He swung the parcel containing the cloth from the back seat, pitched it through the window into her arms and drove off, and Jane turned to find Ellen standing outlined in the great sitting-room window, regarding her fixedly.

As she entered the low-ceilinged room where her aunt was seated in the midst of her old-fashioned possessions Jane found herself transfixed by her furious regard.

'That was Morris Leslie's car you got out of, wasn't it?' she challenged.

'Yes, he drove me home,' Jane admitted, aware of the slight tremble in her voice.

'So you accepted a favour from that brute, that beast!' cried Ellen.

'He insisted,' Jane defended herself. 'He insisted, and somehow I found myself driving home with him, although I told him—'

'Be quiet!' her aunt commanded in a low voice packed with fury. 'You're just like all the rest. He's winning over everyone at Kirtleside: my servant thinks the world of him: Kirstag Bain wants nothing more out of life than that her son should be employed by him. One by one everyone is leaving me and going over to his side. But I didn't think it would happen with you. Now I see you're no better than the rest; a traitor and a betrayer, like the others!'

She stood up and went off to her room with bent shoulders, leaving Jane standing in the silence of the sitting-room.

Slowly Jane climbed the stairs to her room. She opened the parcel and held the cloth before her and gazed at it in the mirror. How beautiful it was! But as she regarded her reflection a bitter taste of self-reproach was in her mouth. Her aunt had complained that by driving home with Morris Leslie, she had betrayed her. What would she say were she to discover that the man she regarded as her enemy had paid for this fabric?

CHAPTER IV

For the next few days Jane found herself flipping through pattern books and magazines with an eye to something suitable for her new dress. Eventually she cut out a design that particularly pleased her from one of the daily papers and set off with it and the fabric for Kirstag Bain's little house.

To her amazement, she found the dressmaker in tears: she had been laid up with a bad cold: her work had fallen behind: she had recently received bills for electricity and gas, and suddenly the gallant little woman felt that it was all too much for her.

'If only Dougal could get back his job with Mr Leslie we'd be able to manage,' Kirstag ended her story, blowing her nose vehemently. 'He has learned his lesson, I can tell you that. And I know Mr Leslie would be pleased with him if he'd only give him another chance—but there, I mustn't bother you with my worries when it's well known what an unforgiving person Mr Leslie is.'

Jane was silent and preoccupied while Kirstag shook

out the material and exclaimed in admiration of its beauty. Then came the business of measuring and the discussion of the pattern, Kirstag exerting herself to speak as cheerfully as possible. It was plain she felt ashamed of airing her sorrows in front of this young girl who was hardly more than a stranger to her. But, as she said, Jane's sympathetic manner had encouraged her to speak out from her heart in a way she would hardly have dared to do even with people who were much longer known to her.

As the little dressmaker chattered on a resolution was forming in Jane's mind: she would go up to Windgates, beard Morris Leslie in his den and ask him to take Dougal Bain back into his employment.

After all, the new owner couldn't *eat* her, Jane was telling herself resolutely as she made her way along the avenue towards that curiously small and narrow door in the middle of the plain, stark façade of the house. In former days the entrances to Scottish houses had deliberately been made narrow so that intruders could easily be repelled, she was thinking wryly. Well, even the door of Windgates would not be small enough to repel *this* invader!

But her heart was beating rapidly as with a certain amount of trepidation she pressed her finger firmly on the bell and waited, holding on as best she could to her resolution.

She was lucky to find him in, she was telling herself as she followed the maid across the narrow hall—but secretly she knew that she had half hoped he would be out so that the moment of her encounter with him might be put off.

She found him in the library, for once in a relaxed mood. He was seated in one of the deep armchairs, and was smoking, pipe in hand, as she was shown in.

'Ah, come away ben,' he greeted her. 'You see, I'm learning the language. Soon I'll be quite acclimatised and no one will know that I haven't lived all my life in Scotland.'

This greeting rather took the wind out of her sails. She had been so set to challenge him and this relaxed easy-going welcome made her feel that the interview was being started off on the wrong foot.

As she took the chair he indicated she was wondering just how she was to broach the difficult subject that had brought her to the house.

She was reminded that her cheeks were flushed and that there had been an obvious air of determination about her as he said, 'And what brings you here—for I don't dare to hope that you've condescended to pay a social call. You know, Jane—may I call you that?— you're inclined to scoff at me as a philistine, but you're a decidedly unsociable body yourself—not at all neighbourly, to my way of thinking. However, enough about that! Something's wrong—that, at least, is plain. Now don't tell me the roof of the factor's house is leaking already or that there's a fault in the electricity, or—'

'I haven't come to ask for anything for myself,' she began so brusquely that a smile flitted across his face.

'No? Then for whom have you come to ask?'

'It's for Dougal Bain. I want you to take him on again. At least—'

'Dougal Bain?' A faint frown crossed his forehead. 'I know whom you're speaking about now: he's the boy who got himself hurt tree felling. His own fault, mind you!'

'But he has learned his lesson,' she assured him.

'Has he, indeed? And what makes you so sure of that? I suppose he told you so himself.'

She had to admit that it was from Mrs Bain's lips that she had heard this.

'Naturally, his mother thinks the best of her son. What woman doesn't? But it wouldn't do if I were as sentimental as that.'

'Will you not do it for his mother's sake?' Jane pleaded. 'She's a fine person and very industrious, but her earnings won't keep two people.'

'So you feel that because Kirstag Bain is a reliable little person I should support that great lazy lout of a son of hers and give him handouts when he lays himself up out of sheer stupidity?'

'But people aren't made to a pattern: some aren't as bright as others: they need time to learn and adjust themselves.'

It was at this point that the door opened and Rhoda Mannering came in. 'Am I interrupting?' she asked brightly.

'No, you've arrived just at the right time. We have a problem here, Jane and I, and perhaps it would be as well to put it up to your arbitration. Jane here feels that Dougal Bain should be taken on again—for his mother's sake, you understand.'

'Dougal Bain! Let me see—you employed him at one time—'

'Yes, the boy who disobeyed orders and got hurt while tree felling,' he remarked.

'The village dressmaker's son,' Rhoda said, and Jane could only marvel at the efficiency of this woman who in the short time she had been at Windgates had already mastered all the details of her employer's intricate affairs. There seemed to be not a name nor a date that she didn't instantly file away in her mind on a first hearing. 'But why should he be taken on again? You paid him compensation while he was ill, didn't you?'

'Yes, I decided to do so—an offering to local goodwill. But Jane feels that this isn't enough. She feels he should be reinstated so that we can go through all this again.'

'But it won't happen again,' Jane told him desperately. 'He's perfectly well and strong now and he has learned his lesson.'

'I doubt if poor Dougal has learned very much,' Morris told her. 'He's the type who will be careless and raise a host of difficulties wherever he is.'

'Well, at least give him a chance!' she cried.

'You see how it is: Kirstag Bain says her son is a reformed character and Jane believes her,' Morris told Rhoda sardonically.

'Naturally his mother is going to recommend the boy,' Rhoda said judiciously.

'Oh, but it's true,' Jane urged.

'Tell us, Rhoda, how do you feel about giving people second chances? Is it a sensible and prudent thing to do, or is it foolishness?' he asked.

'Nowadays, there's no excuse for inefficiency,' Rhoda said coldly. 'I've heard about this boy and certainly *I* wouldn't take him on again were the decision left to me.'

'See what a competent secretary I have,' Morris said with a sort of lazy approval. 'She's been with me only a short time and already she's au fait with all the personalities involved in the business of the estate. I shouldn't be the smallest bit surprised to find she had a dossier on each of them already.'

Rhoda smiled complacently. 'I make it my business to know all about the personalities connected with my work. And as for second chances, I don't believe in them! Those who have proved themselves incompetent should be dismissed—but then I'm not sentimental about people,' she ended with a level challenging glance at Jane.

'So now we have Rhoda's opinion.' Morris puffed at his pipe. 'Into the balance we must put the fact that Mrs Bain herself is a most industrious and competent person. And there is your firm belief, Jane, that Dougal has learned his lesson to be weighed against Rhoda's conviction that people should never be given a second chance. Tell you what, I'll think it over and see what conclusion I come to.'

And with this Jane had to be content.

Somewhat to Jane's surprise, Rhoda accompanied her from the room as she made her departure.

She closed the door of the library carefully behind her, then said, 'You know, you should realise that Morris has already made up his mind not to reinstate Dougal Bain. Other people have applied to him for second chances and in every single case they've been refused. You should tell Mrs Bain to encourage her son to look for employment elsewhere. If this boy were in earnest he would go south to Glasgow and get a job there.'

'Then you definitely won't speak for him?' Jane asked flatly.

Rhoda's eyes met hers for a moment before she said, 'No. No, I won't plead for him. And there's a good reason for that. You see, once during the early years of my career I made a bad mistake. Well, in spite of all my excuses I was dismissed and had to go elsewhere and begin again from the beginning. It was a lesson to me: it taught me that if I weren't efficient, no matter how extenuating the circumstances were, no one would have any mercy on me. I had to swallow my medicine, and I don't see why this boy shouldn't do the same thing. Why should I have pity on him? If I've built up a name for efficiency it's because I've learned that if I make mistakes I must pay for them. And if you feel that this is too hard an outlook on life just remember that experience has taught me the hard facts of life.'

For an instant Jane gazed at her. Rhoda was the picture of the glossy, brittle career woman, but at that moment she felt that to a certain extent she understood her. If she presented a hard surface to the world it was because life had taught her to dissemble.

As Jane went away she felt her spirits droop dismally. It was clear that the secretary was informing her that her mission had met with defeat. Morris had merely been showing politeness in promising to consider the reinstating of Dougal, for Rhoda had told her clearly that, in fact, it was not his practice to give second chances. He had merely been avoiding the embarrassment of having to give her an unequivocal refusal.

So it was that on the occasion of her first fitting for the dress Jane found her footsteps dragging as she approached Kirstag Bain's little house. She had a horrid image of what would be awaiting her when she knocked on the door—Kirstag inwardly dejected, in spite of the artificial brightness of her chatter, because she now knew that Morris Leslie would never give her son employment again.

But when she at last found herself in the gloomy

back room where Kirstag sat amongst her threads and snippets of cloth, she found the little dressmaker radiant.

'The most wonderful news!' she greeted Jane. 'Mr Leslie has taken on Dougal again, and what's more, he has given him light work that he's well fitted for and I feel sure that this time he will make a success of things. And it's all due to your speaking a good word for him. I cannot thank you enough for it and—'

'But are you sure it was because I mentioned your son to Mr Leslie?' Jane interrupted, cutting short the dressmaker's thanks. She had been so completely certain that her visit to Morris Leslie's home had been an utter failure.

'Oh yes, quite sure,' Kirstag assured her. 'He called in to see me the other evening and told me he was taking Dougal back and that it was you I had to thank for it. And indeed I do. I can't say how grateful I am to you. You must have a cup of tea before we fit the dress.'

'Oh no, don't bother,' Jane exclaimed. But already the dressmaker had disappeared to put the kettle on. There was such a radiant smile on her face as she set down a cup and saucer which didn't match and, rummaging in a cupboard, produced a box of biscuits and a couple of baps and began to butter them with an over-lavish hand that Jane hadn't the heart to refuse further. It was so clear that the dressmaker was looking upon this as a way of expressing her gratitude. She chattered away as she made tea.

'You mustn't mind if things are a bit rough and tumble,' she told Jane cheerfully as she cascaded sweet biscuits on to her plate. 'We dressmakers never seem to have time to do any real housekeeping. It's hurry,

hurry, hurry from morning to night and when we do get a few minutes to ourselves, somehow we don't seem to feel like turning to and doing housework.'

The tea which she poured was thick and strong, but Jane sipped it with every sign of enjoyment.

It was the same when, tea over, Kirstag began the fitting of the dress. Jane found that she had added all sorts of little touches such as trimmings and special sewing effects which must have cost time and endless trouble—and again she knew that this had been done to express gratitude.

'Oh yes, I must say I got quite a different impression of Mr Leslie when I met him face to face,' Kirstag was saying as she pinned and tucked, shortened or lengthened and stood back to observe the effect. Jane discovered that Morris Leslie and the wonderful good fortune of her son being employed once more were subjects to which the dressmaker constantly reverted. 'You see, I thought he was all harshness and contempt for those who are not so clever, but he's not like that at all. "You know, I'm somewhat to blame for what happened," he said to me. "I should have known that Dougal wasn't fit for the work he was doing and that he was bound to come to grief sooner or later. But this time I'm putting him on something easier and we'll see how he does." And do you know, I do believe, that this time he will be able to hold down his job and that things will be better for us from now on.' There were tears of happiness in Kirstag's eyes as she spoke.

Jane, listening, could hardly believe her ears. Was this the arbitrary, uncompromising man she had known? The idea that he had done this kindness in response to her pleas for Dougal gave her an uneasy sense of gratitude. The least she could do would be to go and thank him, she thought doubtfully as she made her departure.

She made up her mind to go immediately, before her courage failed her.

When she went up the avenue of Windgates, as always, she paused, peeping through the wrought iron gates leading to the walled garden. Again there was a blaze of colour in the broad herbaceous borders that ran against the walls making a dazzling background to the velvet lawn and the sparkling fountain. Snapdragons, pansies, sweet peas and roses now rioted in place of the spring flowers that had bloomed on that morning when she had first returned to Windgates.

She was standing at the wrought iron gate, dreamily contemplating the scene, her face almost touching the iron scrollwork, when she heard the sound of horses' hooves behind her and, swinging around, she found that Rhoda and Morris were riding towards her around the bend in the avenue. Rhoda, looking superb on a coal black horse, was chatting animatedly to Morris, but as she turned her head and caught sight of Jane her expression changed to one of annoyance which was replaced a moment later by a look of amusement.

' You look just like the " orfling " in the story book, pressing her nose against the pastrycook's window,' she called laughingly as she drew near.

Jane, looking up to these two bright people sitting so high up above her on their magnificent horses, did indeed feel like the ' orfling ' in the fairy story. She felt herself blush uncomfortably as she became aware of Morris regarding her quizzically.

As though guessing her intention he said quietly, ' Don't run away, Jane. I'm extremely flattered that you should think the garden so well worth a visit. It's not everyone who thinks my efforts are worth while. In fact Rhoda is inclined to lecture me about the needless extravagance. Don't you, Rhoda?'

Jane felt a little stab of desolation as she saw him glance across at the girl in obvious admiration. It was not surprising Rhoda should draw a man's eyes, Jane thought. Her cheeks touched with carmine and her eyes sparkling after a gallop, Rhoda looked breathtakingly beautiful, even more so now that the brittle veneer of the confident secretary had slipped a little.

Rhoda shrugged indifferently, 'Frankly I'm not one of those people who go into raptures of enthusiasm over masses of flowers: a little goes a long way, as far as I'm concerned, and keeping these gardens must cost you a packet.' Her voice was cool and detached, but Jane sensed a shrewishness beneath the remark.

Morris raised his eyebrows in mock dismay. ' Don't tell me you're the kind of woman who prefers a solitary orchid to a bouquet of summer flowers?'

Rhoda nodded. 'Actually, I do, though obviously Jane is all for nature in the raw.'

'Well, Jane?' His eyes sought hers. 'For goodness' sake tell me you approve of my efforts, otherwise I'll feel utterly crushed!'

He was laughing at her, she knew, but something defensive rose in her to smother for a moment her overwhelming feeling of being odd man out.

'I love the walled garden,' she said quickly. 'It's so beautiful, I think, because it's hidden behind walls and gates and one has to seek it out. I mean, it's not—not flamboyant, like most gardens,' she ended lamely, feeling Rhoda eyeing her with an acid sweetness.

'You mean you simply walked up the avenue to get a peep at the garden: it certainly shows a dedication to nature! But was that really all you had in mind?' Rhoda asked.

Now that she was being so obviously challenged, Jane recovered her self-possession. She met Rhoda's eyes levelly. 'No, actually, now that you mention it, I also had in mind to speak to Mr Leslie, if you've no objection.'

'Objection?' Rhoda trilled, 'but how could I possibly have an objection, my dear girl? After all, I'm only the humble secretary-cum-dogsbody. Isn't that so, Morris?' She slanted a glance at her employer, her long tawny lashes sweeping her cheeks.

Morris surveyed them both enigmatically and Jane wondered if he suspected the covert duel that lay between their little passage of arms, but he simply said levelly, 'Go on into the library and I'll be with you in a few minutes.'

'Perhaps I could deal with it, whatever it is,' Rhoda put in. 'As you know, I'm pretty well au fait with all the affairs of Windgates by now.'

There was a short silence and again Jane felt herself grow embarrassed. Somehow Rhoda, with her hard self-possession, had the ability to make her feel gauche and naïve and to leave her at a loss for words.

She felt herself on the verge of saying some blundering words when Morris put in smoothly, 'I think perhaps I'll personally see to this matter, Rhoda.'

She shrugged, then swung her mount towards the house. 'Just as you like. But it's time I was getting back to work. Always the efficient secretary.'

As they rode off towards the stables Morris had had built, Jane slowly made her way towards the house.

True to his word, she had been established in the library only a few minutes when he came in with his characteristic brisk step.

Riding clothes suited him, she decided. They rather tended to accentuate his stocky build, but at the same time they emphasised that air of strength and vitality that seemed to emanate from him like an aura.

'Tell me, do you ride?' he opened the conversation with his usual abruptness.

'Not really. I used to amble about on a little donkey when I was a child here when Aunt Ellen was —when Aunt Ellen lived here.'

'A pity. You might have joined us this morning. Rhoda rides well. There's nothing as invigorating as a gallop in the morning; puts you in trim for the rest of the day. But I suppose that's hardly what you've come to discuss!'

'No—' she hesitated. 'I've been at Kirstag's house and she told me you're reinstating Dougal. I—I wanted to thank you.'

'Thank me?' She saw his eyes glitter with amusement. 'So you are assuming that it was your eloquent appeal that turned the scales for Dougal! Hasn't it occurred to you that I may not be quite the ogre you take me for?'

'Oh!' For a moment she was nonplussed. Once again he had managed to make her feel the suppliant, and she felt a growing resentment.

'So you would have taken him back—even if I hadn't asked you? That's what you mean, isn't it?'

For a moment he drummed his fingers thoughtfully on the table. 'Let's say I reconsidered things. You mustn't underestimate your abilities as an advocate, Jane, but it's becoming more and more clear to me that, as far as you're concerned, I'm rather a despot. Perhaps I wanted to show you that I'm not quite the autocrat you believe me to be. After all, you've never made the slightest pretence of liking me, and one grows tired of being regarded as an unrelenting tyrant. Let's say I succumbed to those blue eyes of yours which at this moment are regarding me so earnestly. But don't tell me you visited Kirstag simply to inquire after Dougal's fate! Perhaps the dress for the ceilidh had something to do with it?'

'Well, yes,' she admitted, blinking at the rapid transition of subject.

'And how is it coming along—if a mere male may inquire.'

'I'm very pleased with it,' she told him shyly, remembering that encounter in Aberdeen. Somehow or other she must repay him, she told herself fleetingly.

As though guessing her thoughts, he said, 'Some day I shall demand payment.'

When she did not reply, he went on immediately, 'So you're going to be the belle of the ball—in spite of not knowing how to dance! Well, we must rectify that. You have time for a lesson, I suppose? You needn't return immediately?'

Before Jane had time to reply, Rhoda entered the room. Once more she was dressed in trim elegance. She wore a beautifully cut dress of cream-coloured thin woollen material with deep pockets.

'By the way, Rhoda,' he turned to her, 'we have an extra man on our payroll from now on, Dougal Bain.'

'The dressmaker's son? So you took him back! But why?' Then as Rhoda's glance passed between him and Jane, she added, 'But then you couldn't refuse when Jane asked, could you?' She crossed the room to the big table at which she usually sat and picked up a bundle of papers. 'You promised to give the architect your decision on these plans,' she said, pointedly ignoring Jane. 'He's rung several times and is all impatience for your say-so.'

'Well, he'll just have to wait a while longer,' Morris told her. 'This morning I have important business to attend to.'

'Oh, in that case—'

'Yes, I have to teach Jane how to do Scottish dancing.'

'Oh!' Rhoda flushed with shock and embarrassment. 'I suppose that's much more important than a small matter of business?'

'Yes, in this case it is. All work and no play makes Jack a dull boy. So if you don't mind, Rhoda, please see that I'm not disturbed for the next hour or two.'

Without answering, Rhoda marched out of the room with the bundle of papers under her arm, and shut the door with a decisive little slam of disapproval.

But this display of pique appeared to be unnoticed by her employer. 'I've a few records of pipe music. We'll go into the drawing-room and remove the carpets so as to keep in Mrs MacInnes's good graces, and then set to work. Come on, let's go.' He reached down and, catching Jane by her hands, pulled her to her feet.

Jane hesitated. She had noticed the glittering angry glance Rhoda had directed at her before her departure. Her relationship with the girl, although not particularly friendly, had been at least amicable. But now she realised that things between them would be subtly altered. Rhoda, even though she might hide it by her air of bright and glittering sophistication, resented Morris's friendly overtures towards her and Jane guessed that she was especially put out by the reversal of his plans concerning Dougal Bain.

'Well, what are you waiting for?' Morris asked her quizzically. 'Are you considering whether my offer to teach you Scottish dancing is simply a cover-up for more devious plans?'

'Of course not,' she said hurriedly, and heard him laugh gently as quick colour touched her cheeks.

'Then let's go. What are we waiting for? I've the feeling that you'll make an apt pupil. If so, I want you to do me credit at the ceilidh.'

She followed him to the drawing-room with the certainty that her newfound friendship with Morris Leslie was resented by Rhoda.

Some evenings later, when Jane opened the door to Gregory's ring, she was disconcerted to find that he had a record of ceilidh music under his arm. 'I've come to give you a few tips on ceilidh dancing,' he informed her.

'You must have tea first,' Ellen said firmly, coming up behind them as they stood in the hall. 'Maggie made some potato scones this morning and we're going to toast them and have them simply running with butter as they should be eaten. Now get your jacket off, Gregory, and set to work with that toasting fork while Jane sets the table.'

Jane put out egg cups, then placed a saucepan of brown eggs to boil in the kitchen, catching snatches of conversation between the young doctor and her great-aunt as she went in and out to the table.

'You know, Gregory, I do believe those tablets you gave me are beginning to do my headaches some good,' Ellen was informing him gravely.

'Don't tell me you're actually taking them!' He

raised the fork to examine the potato scone he was toasting with a critical eye and then returned it to the fire for that extra moment or two which would give it that crisp, savoury brownness that would make all the difference.

'Yes, Jane persuaded me to give them a trial,' Ellen was telling him blandly. 'And, mind you, I think they're doing the trick.'

Gregory, adding the toasted scone to the pile on a plate warming before the fire, raised his eyes in self-commiseration in Jane's direction, as she entered the room with a teapot. 'So you're taking them because Jane suggested it! Tell me, just who is the doctor in this district?'

'Jane is a girl with plenty of common sense,' Ellen spoke up for her great-niece. 'I've learned to have great faith in her judgement. I only hope we'll be able to keep her with us as long as possible.'

'Why, is she thinking of leaving us already?'

'Would you believe it, the foolish girl is talking about taking a job in Aberdeen which would mean spending the week there in some horrible little poky flat or bedsitter, and that I should see her only at the week-ends. I wouldn't hear of it for a minute. "We'll manage somehow," I told her. And as long as you don't burn too many of Maggie's potato scones we'll be able to pull through.'

'Oh!' He jerked the fork away from the fire with an exclamation. The scone he had been toasting had actually caught fire and was burning with a bluish flame.

He blew it out with an air of grave attention. 'It would be wonderful if we could keep Jane here at Kirtleside—that is, if she doesn't grow bored with us.'

'It's up to you, Gregory, to see that she doesn't!'
Ellen told him in her blunt way as they took their
seats at the tea-table. 'And that's why I'm so pleased
you're going to this ceilidh. Jane has got a new dress
for it and I must say Kirstag has put herself out to
make a wonderful job of it—such attention to detail
as never was. I'm sure she doesn't put a quarter as
much trouble into anything she does for me.'

'And if she did, you probably wouldn't even notice,'
he told her, laughing. 'You're only making excuses to
grumble, for you know in your heart you don't care
for clothes. But it's not surprising Kirstag put her best
efforts into a dress for you, Jane,' he turned to her.
'The village is ringing with the story that it was
through your influence that Dougal was taken on
again. Dougal, of course, is a no-good—and accident-
prone into the bargain—but his mother is a hardwork-
ing person, and very reliable and trustworthy. It was
a fine thing to do, Jane. But then one doesn't need to
know you long to know you have a kind heart!'

Jane, feeling her great-aunt's eyes upon her, glanced
at him appealingly.

But Gregory, unaware of having made a faux pas,
laughed. 'I can imagine how you tackled him—like
a spitting cat or like a little terrier. I suppose even
Morris Leslie couldn't resist the onslaught.'

It was at this moment that Ellen burst in with,
'What's all this, Jane? Have you been seeing Morris
Leslie behind my back?'

Gregory's expression changed as he saw the look of
consternation on Jane's face. 'If she saw him I'm
sure it was only to plead for Dougal,' he tried to undo
the damage he had done.

But Ellen was not to be placated. 'I'll have no

favours from that man,' she said in a loud, harsh voice. 'A man who cares for nothing but money!'

'That's not so,' Jane defended him. 'He knows Scottish dancing and music and—'

'I wouldn't be under an obligation to him for the world,' Ellen interrupted, 'I'm ashamed of you, Jane, if what Gregory says is true—but perhaps it's all a story.'

She waited in ominous silence, and Jane was forced to admit that she had seen Morris to plead for Dougal's reinstatement.

'I'm sure your intentions were good,' Ellen said, when at last Jane's voice faltered to a halt, 'But I do wish you had consulted me before doing such a thing.'

'I'm sure Jane meant no more than a kindness to Kirstag,' Gregory came to her rescue. 'After all, we can't afford to fight one another, even though we may not agree on every point. I don't approve of him, but I don't quarrel with him on that account. In a small place like this we must pull together or perish, and I think Jane did what was right in trying to help Kirstag, no matter what her personal feelings may be towards Morris.'

'Well, I don't see it that way.' Ellen had risen to her feet and was looking down on Jane with resentful eyes. 'It seems to me that people should have some principles: that they should practise what they preach. I think a bit of good old-fashioned, stiff-necked Scottish pride would do us no harm—the spirit that asked no favours and that spoke its mind without fear or favour. I'm sorry to say this, Jane, but I think the less of you for what you have done.'

In stiff dignity the old lady turned away and went towards her bedroom, leaving Jane and Gregory in silence in the cosy sitting-room.

'I'd better go to her,' Jane said miserably. 'She's upset—and I don't blame her.'

'Better leave her for a moment or two until she cools down,' Gregory said. 'She's quick-tempered, but she won't keep it up. You'll find it easier to speak to her in a little while. Come, let's put this record on and I'll show you a few of the dance steps.'

He folded aside the rug before the fire and put the record on the old-fashioned record player, and in a few moments the toe-tapping sound of ceilidh music sounded through the room. 'This is how it goes,' he began. He danced a few steps, then held out his hands to her. 'Come along, just copy me: you'll be into it in no time.'

But Jane made no move. 'It's all right, Gregory,' she told him. 'I know how to do it.'

He paused, regarding her, the animation fading from his face. 'You know the steps? But who taught you?'

Then, as she did not reply, he went on, 'You were saying at tea that Morris Leslie knows Scottish dancing. Is it possible that it was he who taught you?'

As Jane nodded, he walked over to the record-player and shut off the music. 'You know, Jane, perhaps there is something in Ellen's attitude after all. I admit I'm not disinterested in what I'm about to say, but there's also the fact that Morris Leslie is a hard, ruthless man. He can be charming when he wants to win people to his side, but underneath is nothing but self-interest.'

As she made no reply he turned away abruptly. 'But there, you're hardly likely to take my words very seriously when you know that they're inspired by the green-eyed monster.'

Later, when Gregory had gone, Jane made her way towards Ellen's room and knocked softly on the door.

At Ellen's call, she went in and found the old lady standing at the wide window staring out unseeingly.

Slowly, Ellen came forward and seated herself in the low, cushioned, white-painted basket chair. 'You know, Jane, I've been thinking about you,' she began, 'and it's obvious that you can't go back to that step-mother of yours. It's unthinkable. There's nothing for you to do but stay here with me. Some day you're going to marry, and it's wonderful to know that you're getting on so well with Gregory. I don't know where you'd find a finer young fellow. I've known him since he was a child—knew his father before him—yes, and his grandfather before him again. He comes of good sound stock and you'd go far and fare worse before you found his like.'

'But I don't love him,' Jane burst out unthinkingly.

Her aunt's lips tightened ominously and Jane went on, 'To me, marriage isn't simply a matter of convenience. I must be in love with the man I'm going to marry.'

'You'd care for Gregory soon enough if it weren't for this Morris character,' Ellen said abruptly. 'You've been meeting him behind my back—after all I've told you about him.'

'But what has he done that's so dreadful?' Jane protested. 'After all, he's built you this house and has paid—has seen that Maggie comes in to see to your wants and—and—he's not altogether bad,' she ended desperately. 'He's done a lot of good things too.'

'So that's how it looks to you,' Ellen said grimly, after a moment's silence. 'I can see it's time I spoke out and let you know exactly how matters stand. I forbid you to have anything to do with Morris Leslie because the man's a thief.'

'A thief?' Jane faltered. 'What do you mean?'

'I mean that he robbed me; bought Windgates for a mere song.'

'But you're able to live on the money you got for the house,' Jane said weakly after a moment.

'Yes, and how am I living—in penury!' cried Ellen. 'I should have got far more for the property, but he traded on the fact that I was old and unused to business. He and his clever lawyers used every trick in the trade to defraud me of what I should have got.'

'Oh—I didn't know,' Jane said after a moment or two. Somehow, what her aunt was telling her didn't fit in with the character of the man she had come to know a little since her arrival in Kirtleside, yet not for a moment did she doubt the truth of what Ellen was saying.

'You were deceived by that charm of his which he can put on as easily as another man would put on his jacket,' Ellen told her. 'And that's why I'm telling you this, although it's not a thing I'm proud of—it makes me seem too much of a fool, and there's still a bit of pride in the last of the Fergusons which makes me hate to show myself up in such a bad light.'

'I'm sorry,' Jane said with compunction. 'I didn't understand, and—'

'No, you thought I was a neurotic old lady, driven almost crazy by the loss of what had been hers for so long. But no one likes to be robbed—especially of something as dear as one's old home. Remember, Windgates has been in the Ferguson family for centuries.'

'I didn't think—' Jane began contritely. She stopped, overwhelmed with the thought of her disloyalty to her aunt in her growing friendship with the man who had usurped her place at Windgates.

' As to his building this home for me,' Ellen went on heatedly, ' he was more or less forced to do so by public opinion. The Fergusons are still loved and revered in Kirtleside, and in spite of all my faults, they look upon me as the last of the old line. It's my opinion he hoped to establish himself in the district by showing that he had no intention of treating me badly. He guessed I'd be too proud ever to reveal the straits he has reduced me to—pinching and scraping in my old age! Oh, he's very smart is Mr Morris Leslie! He knew that the old clan loyalty is there under the skin and that the people would have resented seeing me reduced to open poverty. He hoped by these tricks to ingratiate himself in the district, and be accepted—not that he ever will be, for he's an outsider and the people will never take to him. But that's what he hoped for.'

As Ellen ceased, there was a long silence in the room. Jane's thoughts were filled with bitter self-reproach. So this was the man she had allowed herself to be cajoled by! She had been willing to meet his overtures more than half way—in spite of all Ellen had hinted at—for the old lady had been too proud to come out directly with the cause of her enmity. But in future she would make certain to show him clearly on which side her loyalties lay. In fact, she would keep out of his way as much as possible.

CHAPTER V

About a week later, as Jane was walking towards the end of the path that led from Ellen Ferguson's house and connected with the main avenue, she was over-taken by Rhoda driving a brown and maroon car. As she drew abreast the secretary leaned out. ' If you're not going anywhere particularly interesting would you care to come along to the station? I'm driving down there now.'

For an instant Jane hesitated, but Rhoda sounded so unusually affable that she felt inclined to accept—and anyway, as Rhoda had suggested, she was not going anywhere in particular. The day was hot and the drive in the open car would be welcome. Nodding acquiescence, she slipped into the seat in front.

' It's really much too hot for walking, isn't it?' Rhoda said pleasantly, as the car slid along the drive, and the cool air riffled through her long, silky hair.

She turned the car into the road and picked up speed. ' This is the sort of agreeable perquisite that goes with a job of this type. Here am I driving through the countryside on a fine summer's day on my way to meet my extremely fascinating boss.'

' You mean you're meeting Morris Leslie!' Jane exclaimed sharply. Since her revealing conversation with Ellen she had decided to steer clear of the auto-cratic owner of Windgates.

Rhoda shot her a glance. ' You sound as if the idea of seeing my respected boss doesn't altogether fill you with bliss.'

' No, it doesn't,' Jane replied shortly. ' In fact, if I'd known you were meeting him I shouldn't have come in the first place.'

For a moment she wondered if she had only imagined the look of satisfaction that flitted across Rhoda's classic features. ' Indeed, and may I ask why you appear to dislike him so much? Personally I get on with him very well. Oh, I'm not saying he's an angel, by any means, for he can be extremely dictatorial when he chooses to be. But then that's how I like my men—with a mind of their own. I'm really awfully glad I decided on this job. If I were in town, I'd be stuck in some stuffy office with no chance of a bit of variety. Of course, it was a gamble in the first place—but it came off, thank goodness, and has turned out even better than I hoped. Although, truth to tell, being secretary to Morris Leslie is by no means a sinecure: he keeps you on your toes. But I'm thoroughly enjoying myself, I admit. It's interesting and varied, and he's giving me more and more responsibility, keeping only the major decisions to himself. In fact, I've had unbelievable luck. He's a fascinating person, as well as being a fine employer.'

Jane glanced at Rhoda's clearly chiselled profile for a moment, nonplussed as to why the secretary should be unburdening herself: somehow these intimate confidences seemed out of character, coming from a person as cool and detached as Rhoda. But she set her lips tightly. She had no intention of revealing to Rhoda what Ellen had confided concerning Morris Leslie.

'All right, so you're keeping your own counsel,' Rhoda laughed a little acidly. 'But as far as I'm concerned, this is the sort of job that suits me down to the ground.'

For a moment silence lay between them and Jane was quite unprepared when Rhoda said abruptly, 'You like him too, don't you, in spite of the stiff-necked attitude you're taking. I always distrust girls when they appear to dislike a man. It usually means they're head-over-heels in love—at least, that has been my experience.'

93

So this, then, was the reason for Rhoda's uncharacteristic affability! She was intent upon establishing an atmosphere in which Jane would have no choice but to reciprocate and be equally forthcoming.

'From what I've heard he doesn't seem to be a particularly admirable character,' Jane said. 'And after all, it's difficult to judge a person when you've met them only a few times.'

'Admirable character!' Rhoda scoffed. 'Don't give me that stuff. No, really, Jane, you don't take me in in the slightest. And as for not seeing much of him—well, really, that sounds strange coming from you, for you always seem to be calling at the house on some pretext or other. Take, for instance, the Dougal Bain affair! You certainly made an impact on that occasion, because Morris is not a man who is easily influenced, I can tell you that much.'

She swung the car around a bend in the road, her slim hands skilful on the wheel, and when Jane made no rejoinder, she went on, 'You know, in lots of ways, I could be extremely helpful to Morris. Women employees are no longer the downtrodden underlings that they used to be in times gone by. Nowadays secretaries make decisions and are socially aware. Although I do say so, I've taught myself to be clever about dress and all those little things that make such a difference to an up-to-the-moment man like Morris. If it should happen that he came to care for me I could be really useful to him in his social as well as his business life, which is just as it should be in marriage. Don't you agree?'

As Jane was casting around in her mind for some rejoinder to these extraordinary confidences, Rhoda went on swiftly, 'Gregory Shields is more in your age group, isn't he? He certainly seems to be a very nice sort of person. Do you like him? Or am I being too nosey? But it's simply that I've always been in the habit of speaking my mind, and the devil take the consequences.'

Jane glanced again at that lovely, clear-cut profile. The drift of Rhoda's remarks was only too clear. She was being quietly warned away from Morris and as good as being ordered to fix her attentions on Gregory.

Her reaction was to maintain a stubborn silence.

'Now I have been nosey and you're offended, isn't that it?' Rhoda asked gently, 'but honestly, I didn't mean to be pushy. It's simply that I naturally take an interest in your affairs. After all, we live so near, we're bound to see quite a lot of each other, aren't we?'

Her conciliatory attitude disarmed Jane. 'Well, yes,' she agreed grudgingly, 'I do like Gregory very much, but there's a great difference between liking and loving.'

'Did I say anything of love?' Again Rhoda gave her tinkling trill. 'Frankly I'm rather a cynic when it comes to men. But liking is quite a good basis on which to start out, and I'd say Gregory likes you more than a little. I've seen him look at you with that certain something in his eye. Don't you think that if you put your mind to it you could like him more than just a little?'

As Jane maintained an uncomfortable silence Rhoda laughed softly, 'All right, why don't you say it, I'm an incorrigible busybody.'

But Jane got the impression that Rhoda had interpreted her silence as acquiescence and was quite satisfied with the results of her probing, for she pressed her foot upon the accelerator with an air that was as good as an inaudible sigh of satisfaction.

She was humming softly to herself as the car whispered through the gravel of the station yard. As she turned off the engine, the train was just drawing into the station and Jane could not help the wry thought that it was typical of Rhoda that her timing had been expert. This was the kind of efficiency, she felt sure, that had rocketed her into a position of trust to Morris Leslie. Had she herself been given this assignment, she would probably have been far too early, or just that little bit too late, which would mean that Morris would be waiting impatiently on the platform while she hurried forward, flustered and apologetic.

There was nothing, of course, flustered about Rhoda as she leaned her slim forearms on the wheel and surveyed the few people who were getting off the train. There were the usual women in neat tweed suits, who had obviously been on shopping trips to town. Then suddenly Morris was approaching them, and Jane wondered why her heart seemed to accelerate at the sight of his strong, broad-shouldered figure.

' You don't mind slipping into the back seat, do you, Jane?' Rhoda asked smoothly as he drew near to the car. ' I've lots of business things to discuss with him and I know you'll understand.'

And before she quite knew how it happened, Jane found herself seated in solitary state in the back seat. She was only half listening as Rhoda and Morris spoke of the business of the estate. It was a subject that had no possible bearing on her life and she felt no interest in their discussion as she watched the countryside flit by. She lay disconsolately back against the soft leather cushions feeling utterly alone and out of things.

It was only as they reached Windgates that she

realised that, as far as Morris Leslie was concerned, she was no longer to be the passive listener.

Rhoda had driven up to the door, still chatting affably and obviously revelling in her role as the confident secretary, and it was clear that it came as a shock to her when, as she drew to a halt, Morris said abruptly, 'And now we must discover what's troubling Jane. She has maintained what I can only describe as a marked silence since we left the station and I can only presume that, in some way or other, I've been to blame.'

'But what utter nonsense!' Rhoda laughed dismissively. 'Why on earth should you imagine such a thing just because a girl happens to be a little dreamy?'

What she was really saying, Jane thought resentfully, was what possible reason could the lowly Jane Talbot have to be resentful of the high and mighty Morris Leslie, master of Windgates.

'Anyway, Morris, I've lots of things to discuss with you and I'm sure Jane's bored stiff and dying to get away.'

'Indeed?' Morris returned grimly. 'Well, whether she is or not she's going to remain until I get to the bottom of things.'

But Jane had already decided upon the line she would take with this despot. She opened the door. 'Aunt Ellen is expecting me,' she said coldly. 'I'll walk back, thank you.'

'Oh no,' he gritted, and before she knew quite what had happened to her Jane found her arm being taken firmly in a hard, ruthless grasp and she was pulled out of the car. 'Don't think you're getting off as easily as that. You're coming with me, young lady. You've some explaining to do. After all, you've maintained a disgruntled silence ever since we left the station and I think it's only right I should have an explanation.'

' But I don't owe you any explanation,' Jane retorted sulkily, and was surprised to find Rhoda swiftly come to her rescue.

' She's right, you know, Morris. You're being ridiculous. Of course Jane needn't explain herself to you. Anyway, we've loads of business to discuss. Actually I've only skimmed the top because I knew you'd be tired after your journey. Let's go into the library and get down to things after Mrs McInnes has given you a meal. I'll get her to fix sandwiches and coffee if you feel like nothing heavier. After we've ironed things out you'll feel a lot better.'

' Thanks, Rhoda,' Morris retorted dryly, ' but even with Mrs MacInnes' ministrations I don't expect to feel better until I've discovered what the marked silence is all about.'

Jane felt his fingers again bite ruthlessly into her arm.

' Go ahead into the library, Rhoda. I'll join you later. This young lady and I have things to discuss and I don't intend to be put off any longer.'

' Oh.' Rhoda hesitated, the colour in her cheeks heightening at this uncompromising dismissal. ' Oh, very well, if that's what you want,' she concluded docilely.

' That's what I do want,' Morris said grimly, and Rhoda, without another word, opened the library door and disappeared.

' Now, young lady, kindly explain what the sulks are about.'

' I'm not sulking,' Jane retorted, stung to the quick at this bland dismissal of her righteous indignation.

' You're coming with me and you're going to give an explanation of why you're taking this attitude.'

Before she quite knew how it had happened, Jane found herself being propelled firmly into the house. She gazed up at him resentfully, but found her eyes wavering uncertainly as she met his steely regard.

' Now, just explain yourself, young lady. What's all this about? Don't think for a moment that I'll let you go until I get a convincing explanation.'

' All right, if you must know,' she burst out, ' Aunt Ellen has been telling me how little you gave her for Windgates. You took a mean advantage when you know how dreadful things were for her, and I despise and loathe you for it!'

' So you despise and loathe me, do you?' She gave a little gasp as his fingers bit into her arm. ' Well, for a change you're going to listen to me. It's time you realised what condition Windgates was in when I took it off your aunt's hands.'

' What do you mean?' she gasped as he drew her unrelentingly further into a part of the house which she had not entered since childhood.

' No, you're coming with me,' he gritted. ' I'm going to show you just what a bargain I'm supposed to have made.'

Jane found herself being propelled up the broad staircase and catapulted into one of the bedrooms.

She gazed about her, and for a moment she forgot her resentment at his cavalier behaviour as she let her eyes roam about the room with blank dismay. This was the bedroom she had slept in so many years ago, but it had been a gracious room then, with its gleaming furniture; its carved Victorian bed, damask hangings and thick carpeting. But what had come over it in the interim? she wondered bleakly, for the heavy embossed wallpaper billowed from the walls and the ornate plaster ceiling was stained with damp and grimed with dust. She stood silent and dismayed as she saw the deterioration that the years had wrought.

But she had barely time to observe all the details before she was dragged from one room to the other, each showing unmistakable signs of neglect and decay.

' Well, what do you think of my fine bargain now?' he demanded as, breathlessly, Jane found herself dragged to a halt in one of the smaller rooms. It too reeked of damp and neglect. 'Do you still feel that your aunt was tricked out of her inheritance, or are you prepared to review your opinion of the robber baron from Canada?'

Jane drew in her breath. It was impossible to express how appalled she felt by this deterioration in Windgates. Somehow she had always remembered it as it had been in her childhood, calm and gracious, with highly polished furniture, giving the impression that as the years would roll by, it would always retain its air of durability and permanency. She felt tears spring to her eyes. What hideous changes had overcome the old house since her childhood? It was not surprising that Morris Leslie had offered what her aunt considered such a small sum for the wreck of a once gracious home. Yet, perversely, all her sympathies now lay with Aunt Ellen. Covertly she tried to wipe away the tears, conscious that Morris's eyes were relentlessly fixed on her.

' Poor Aunt Ellen,' she said at last, ' she was always such an orderly person. I can't imagine how she let things get into such a state of dilapidation! When I was young things were so different.'

'When you were young!' Did she only imagine it, or had the harshness died from his voice? 'Tell me, Jane, what room did you sleep in?'

'The one you showed me first, with the high carved bed.'

'I see, then I must try to imagine you there at night, very small and lonely beneath the high, brocaded bed-board, the moon, perhaps, shining through the window and touching your hair with silver.'

His voice had definitely lost its harsh timbre and for the first time she heard the pulsating softness that made her feel extremely vulnerable. He had drawn close to her, his masculinity overwhelming her resistance.

'Tell me, what did you dream of in those days?' he asked gently. 'Did you imagine, perhaps, that in the future you would meet someone who would bring you happiness?'

She drew back defensively as she felt his arms engulf her. 'No, of course not, I was only a child. Why should I imagine such things?' But as she said the words she knew them to be untrue. Even then, in spite of her aunt's disapproval, she had often stolen quietly downstairs and collected from the bookcase novels of romance and chivalry and read them happily in the depths of her broad, soft bed by the light of a huge golden-shaded oil-lamp.

'All right, why don't you admit it?' he insisted. 'What was he like, this romantic lover who was to ride out of the woods towards you on his caparisoned palfrey? Was he dark or fair? Did he wear a silver helmet?'

Jane shook her head, loath to tell him that, in her childish dreams, she had always imagined a dark-avised stranger riding up to claim her, someone not unlike Morris himself, with his swarthy colouring and deep-set mocking eyes.

'All right,' he laughed gently, his hands touching her cheeks, 'so you don't believe in revealing your dreams, do you? Very well, I shan't force you, but somehow I have the foolish idea that your hero was not a blond Sir Lancelot.'

When she still didn't reply, he said, 'Very well, I shall be the " parfit, gentil knight " for a change and, incongruously enough, instead of offering to do battle for your sweet sake with your favour waving in my helmet, I shall offer you tea in the library.'

For a moment she gazed at him in bewilderment. She had been carried away by his words, reliving again a dream she had had in childhood. Then, suddenly, they both burst into laughter and, hand in hand, were running down the stairway.

Amusement still lay between them as they reached the library. As they entered, Rhoda looked up idly. She reclined regally on a broad leather chair. Beside her on the trestle table stood a silver tray, piled with sandwiches and petits fours, and as her eyes fell on their clasped hands, she pulled herself upright, her eyes narrowing. But her voice was languid as she said, 'Hello, Morris. I told Mrs MacInnes to let us have tea. I suppose it was quite in order.'

'But of course. There's nothing we'd like better. Am I right, Jane?'

As she saw the direction in which Rhoda's eyes turned, Jane withdrew her hand from Morris's hurriedly.

'But tea has been brought only for us, Morris. I didn't realise that Jane would be here,' Rhoda said sharply.

'Then perhaps Mrs MacInnes won't find it too much of a chore to provide us with another cup and saucer,' Morris said easily.

Rhoda shrugged and crossed to the porcelain Victorian bell set into the wall. 'But of course! It was my fault in the first place. I simply didn't know Jane was staying on.'

'But of course you didn't,' Morris replied, and Jane wondered if she didn't detect a certain irony in his words. 'I've been showing Jane just how dilapidated things had become since she left Windgates. I don't think she had realised quite what changes had occurred since she was a child here.'

'Oh, is that what you were doing?' Rhoda sounded relieved and Jane wondered if this explanation eradicated her dismay at seeing their hands clasped so closely as they entered the room.

It was at this point that the maid opened the door. 'You rang, Miss Mannering?' she inquired.

'Yes,' Rhoda said easily. 'We've Miss Talbot for tea. I didn't realise she would be staying on.'

For an instant the girl's eyes flashed towards Jane with unflattering perspicacity. 'I shan't be a moment, miss,' she said obsequiously as she closed the door behind her.

So already the staff were regarding Rhoda as their future mistress, Jane thought dismally. But then why shouldn't they, for as Rhoda had so recently pointed out, she was eminently suited to be the mistress of Windgates, whereas she herself was so obviously a misfit.

Suddenly she wished heartily that she had not accepted Morris's offer of tea but had, instead, slipped quietly back to her aunt's house, for already she could detect between Rhoda and Morris a quiet, subtle understanding that once again filled her with discomfort as the outsider.

Jane was unusually quiet that evening as she sat with Ellen in the small sitting-room and tried to concentrate on a book, while Ellen busily knitted. She had plenty to consider in connection with her conversation with Rhoda in the car that afternoon. So Rhoda was already setting her cap at Windgates and Morris Leslie! The future she was planning for herself was only too easy to visualise. She would be a competent, charming and gracious hostess to the wealthy people whom Morris would attract to this spot and Jane had reluctantly to admit to herself that Rhoda seemed ideally suited to the position of Morris's wife. She did not doubt for an instant that Rhoda's glossy sophistication, combined with her amazing grasp of detail, and her tireless energy, would make her an ideal partner for the new owner of Windgates.

But eventually it was time to go upstairs to dress for the ceilidh, and as Jane put on her new dress, she knew that all Kirstag's efforts had been worth while, because it was perhaps the most beautiful thing she had ever worn. The rich, glowing orange and gold seemed to deepen the brown of her hair and brought a sparkle to her eyes, and as she turned in front of the mirror before going down, she knew that it was a great success.

As she entered the sitting-room Ellen looked up from her knitting, put her spectacles aside and viewed her with frank appraisal. 'Well, I must say I'm glad I insisted on this, Jane. The Ferguson family may be down, but we're not out—not while you look so lovely. I'm really proud of you. And to think that you've achieved that with the help of the village dressmaker and a few yards of cheap fabric! It just shows you that you needn't be a millionaire's wife to dress well: all you need is natural good looks and a little bit of taste in what you choose.'

Jane stood before her, tongue-tied and guilty. She didn't dare to tell Ellen how expensive this lovely fabric had been, and she shuddered at the idea of explaining just how it had transpired that Morris Leslie had paid for it.

She felt a sense of relief when Gregory came in and her aunt's attention was distracted. It was only too clear from his expression as he listened to Ellen with only half an ear that he, too, thought her new dress a great success, and it was with a glow of happiness that she took her place beside him in the little blue car.

Dancing had already begun when they arrived and as they joined in, Jane, after some nervousness, was pleased to find that she was remembering Morris's instructions and that she was able to take her place in a set without making too many mistakes in the steps. She found the insistent beat of the music and the energetic dancing pretty exhausting and when one of the dances came to an end she laughingly mopped her brow with her handkerchief.

'Thirsty work, this,' Gregory grinned. 'We're badly in need of refreshment. Take a chair here and I'll be back in a jiffy with something to drink.'

He disappeared into the crowd and Jane looked around with interest from her seat beside the wall. She was a little surprised to see how many old people were present, seated in places of honour at the top of the small hall, gossiping and smoking and enjoying jokes between themselves and observing everything with bright old eyes. Evidently the ceilidh was a social event for the whole village, irrespective of age.

'Well, I must say your dancing does credit to my tuition.'

Jane swung around with a little gasp of surprise to find that she had been so engrossed in her observations that she had not noticed Morris slip into the seat beside her. He was wearing a kilt and Jane wondered if he realised how Scottish dress emphasised his broad shoulders and sturdy build.

'I didn't think you'd come,' she exclaimed before she had time to consider. No, not for a moment had she imagined that Morris Leslie would attend such an insignificant occasion as the local ceilidh.

'And why not? Do you think I could possibly miss the first public performance of my one and only pupil, especially when you proved such an apt one. What made you think I wouldn't turn up, Jane?'

'Oh, I don't know,' she stammered. 'It was simply that—that you're always such a busy person. I couldn't see you in this background, somehow.'

'And how exactly do you see me, Jane?' he asked.

She heard the amusement in his voice and considered carefully before she replied. 'Oh, I don't know. Probably as a sort of tycoon, wrapped up all day in business affairs and with very little time for social life—especially for such a small affair as this!'

For a moment there flitted through her mind the picture of Rhoda alone at Windgates and she wondered what the secretary's reaction had been when she had discovered that her high-and-mighty employer was going to spend his evening at the local ceilidh.

'Hasn't it occurred to you, Jane, that I might enjoy such simple recreations? I think you've built up in your mind an image of me that is entirely false. You must remember that in the old days the Leslies were simply humble crofters.'

She looked at the strong, imperious features and, in spite of herself, gave a little laugh of disbelief.

'Why are you laughing?'

'Oh, it's just that I don't see you in the role of the humble crofter.'

'Then how do you see me?'

For a moment she paused, loath to tell him just how importantly he figured in her life.

Then, as though guessing her reluctance, he said quietly, 'It's hot in here, isn't it? What about our slipping out for a breath of air?' He indicated a door at the back of the hall.

'Gregory has gone for drinks,' she put in hurriedly. How quickly she had forgotten Gregory's existence, she reproached herself.

'We won't go far from the door,' Morris urged, 'so when he comes back he'll be able to find us easily.'

Jane hesitated, then stood up. It was certainly stifling in the hall, but she realised that this was a mere excuse. She longed beyond everything to be alone with Morris Leslie.

As they stepped through the doorway she drew in her breath with a little gasp of pleasure, for unexpectedly she found herself in a lovely rose garden in which other couples were strolling.

'Are you surprised?' Morris asked. 'This ceilidh is being held in what was once the old schoolhouse before it was closed up and the children sent into the next village. But the last schoolmaster was a gifted botanist and gardener and made this paradise out of what was no more than a bleak patch of wilderness when he came to it first.'

'How do you know all these things?' she asked curiously.

'You mean tycoons shouldn't have time in their lives for such information?' he asked, and uncomfortably she realised that to a certain extent he must have sensed the awe with which she looked on him.

'It's just that I don't know how you've managed to get to know even the smallest details of life in the village. I mean, you always seem to be so busy.'

'Perhaps it's because Kirtleside is really more important to me than anything else.'

'You mean to make your permanent home here, don't you?' Jane asked impulsively.

He didn't answer and Jane could hear his long strides crunching on the gravel path. Had her question sounded impertinent to him? she wondered, and was glad that the darkness hid the sudden colour that rose to her cheeks.

But his next words filled her with relief.

'Now what makes you say that?' And she knew from his voice that he was quietly smiling.

It gave her courage to continue. 'Oh, it's just that in spite of your air of detachment you know so much about everyone at Kirtleside. You've been here only a comparatively short time, yet already you know nearly all the people and a great deal of the history of its inhabitants—even those who lived here before you came. You knew about this garden, for instance. Apart from that, you've discovered in some way or another everyone's particular problems. You went to the trouble of visiting Kirstag and letting her know you were taking on Dougal again. I mean, why should you do such a thing unless you intended settling here, making your life a part of Kirtleside?'

'I see, so you've thought it all out, my little flatterer,' he said dryly. 'Has it not occurred to you that my conduct may not be as altruistic as you imagine? Have you forgotten I'm a business man in the first instance? Perhaps my seeming benevolence is simply to ensure that I shall have the goodwill of the village for my plans concerning the chalets. You're a very romantic girl, aren't you, Jane? Does every man who appears in your life ride up in shining armour?'

She glanced at him briefly and looked away, loath that he should read her heart. No, only you, Morris, she thought, and was glad that the soft dusk of the evening hid her expression.

She felt his arm steal about her waist. 'Don't you realise, Jane, what an extraordinarily comforting person you are?'

'I'm simply saying what I feel about you,' she told him. 'I suppose that to you it must seem naïve and foolish, the sort of thing that women shouldn't say to men—'

She stopped as she felt his arm tighten like an iron bar about her. The moon broke through the clouds and at last she stole a glance at him and could read the expression in his dark eyes. She felt her heart beat faster as his eyes bored into hers.

'Dear Jane, do you realise how lovely you look?' he said harshly.

'Lovelier than the sophisticated women you've met in your life?' She tried to keep her voice light, but realised the wryness of her tones.

'To me you're much lovelier, because you have so

much more to offer than mere looks. Suddenly you've made my plans seem worth while. Can you understand what a wonderful thing that is for a man?'

'It must be the effect of the moonlight.' She tried to keep her voice even, although she could feel her throat tighten. He would kiss her in a moment, she felt sure. Now was the time to turn back towards that lighted doorway in which she could see a solitary figure outlined. Gregory! He would offer her no problems, she realised. Now was the time to return to him. But she knew she couldn't. She felt impelled to stroll along with Morris into the patch of shade cast by a huge bush covered with yellow blossoms. Perhaps then she would turn back, but not until then.

As she had known he would, he drew her towards him. For a long moment their lips met under the light that filtered through the buttercup-yellow blossoms.

It was only when Gregory's voice called nearby, 'Where are you, Jane?' that they pulled apart.

'This is all my fault,' Morris said easily, as Gregory appeared before them, carrying two glasses. 'It was simply stifling in the hall and I suggested we go out for a walk.'

Jane was silent. Had Gregory seen them, she wondered, as they had merged together in that close and passionate kiss?

'I'm sorry, Gregory,' she said timorously as she took the glass he offered her, 'but as Morris said, it was so hot, and we didn't mean to move far from the doorway.'

'I apologise,' Gregory sounded bitter. 'I can see Morris was keeping you entertained.'

'No, not really,' Morris answered easily. 'I'm afraid

when it comes to entertaining ladies I'm at a sad loss.'

'Don't underestimate yourself.' Gregory's voice was acid. 'I'm not exactly blind. I can see that Jane hasn't been particularly bored by your company.'

'And what exactly do you mean by that?' Morris asked. His voice was mild, but Jane could see how his eyes glittered dangerously in the moonlight.

Silence lay for a moment between the two men, but it was as taut and dangerous as the edge of a dagger and Jane felt her heart beat anxiously at the enmity between the two men, that had burst into flame as suddenly as a bush fire.

Later, as Jane danced again with Gregory, she caught a glimpse of Morris talking animatedly to Kirstag, who was seated amongst the onlookers. On Kirstag's face was a look of delight as her eyes followed her son, Dougal, who seemed to be an excellent dancer and very popular with the girls of the district. For that evening, at least, the little dressmaker was relaxing from her grinding labours, secure in the knowledge that she and her son were under the powerful patronage of the new owner of Windgates.

Gregory turned his head to follow the direction of her eyes and his lips tightened. 'You're bored?' he suggested.

'No, of course not,' she protested.

But in fact she was, and as the evening passed and she no longer glimpsed Morris she guessed that he must have gone home.

'I really think we ought to go, Jane. It's plain you're bored. Why don't you admit it? And frankly, I am too.'

In silence they moved out to his car and as they drove towards Windgates, he said bitterly, 'We were

111

enjoying ourselves this evening until Morris Leslie put in an appearance. At first you were happy in my company. After he arrived everything was ruined. But then that's his way! He destroys everything he touches. Nothing will do him but that every eye should be upon him. You were quite a different girl after that walk with him in the garden. He kissed you, didn't he? Don't take me for an utter fool! I could see something had happened.'

'Gregory!' Jane laid her hand for an instant upon the sleeve of his jacket as he drove. 'Don't take it so seriously. It was just that the hall was too hot, so we went out. I hadn't realised how energetic Scottish dancing could be. It was a sort of accident. A kiss in the moonlight means nothing to him—nor to me either, so don't let's bother ourselves about it.'

She felt her heart sink as she spoke. By explaining it, she had simplified it to herself. Yes, that was how it must have appeared to Morris. A moonlit night, a pretty girl in his arms, nothing more!

'Was it like that?' Gregory was asking, a note of eagerness in his voice that smote her.

'Cross my heart and wish to die,' she told him cheerfully.

By the time they reached Ellen's house their pleasant relationship was restored. They strolled across the patch of smooth lawn before the sitting-room window, and suddenly his arms were about her and he was kissing her.

He shouldn't have chosen that moment, was the thought that flashed through Jane's mind—not when the memory of Morris's kiss was so vivid in her mind. Gregory was a fine person: she liked him very much, and had Morris Leslie not been on the horizon, who knew but that she could have found it in her heart to care for him deeply. But Morris was there, and she could not but compare her reaction to Gregory's kiss and the storm of feeling that had swept her in Morris's embrace.

Jane felt in the tiny silk purse hanging from her wrist and took out her key. 'You'll come in for a drink?' she invited.

'No, thanks.' His voice sounded grave in the dark. 'Not this evening. I've been lucky tonight and don't want to spoil the magic.'

CHAPTER VI

As Jane came out of the post office a few mornings later she saw Rhoda's elegant brown and maroon car parked outside Kirstad's little house. A moment later Rhoda herself appeared and, seeing Jane, waved to her. 'Are you going to Windgates?' she asked, as Jane approached. 'Would you like me to drive you back?'

The weather was very sultry and Jane gladly accepted the offer of a lift.

As she got in Rhoda said rather wryly, 'Imagine, I've had to get Kirstag to let out one of my skirts. I seem to have put on pounds and pounds since I came to Kirtleside. I must say I blame it on Mrs MacInnes. She's so keen to show Morris how excellently she can supply him with Scottish cooking that we seem to live on such things as Scotch broth, haggis, shortbread and black bun. And I suppose I needn't tell you what food like that can do to one's figure? Morris simply adores ye olde Scottish cooking, and he never seems to put on as much as a pound, but then his is an active life, while I'm mostly engaged on sedentary work. I'm sure I must be getting as heavy as the fat woman in a sideshow.'

This was, of course, deliberate exaggeration on Rhoda's part. She was looking for reassurance, Jane realised, yet now when she regarded the girl closely, she could not but admit that she had indeed gained weight lately. The outlines of the once svelte figure had, owing to the fare at Windgates, become slightly blurred.

Before she realised the effect her words would have, her natural honesty made her blurt out ingenuously, 'Well, you're not exactly fat, Rhoda, but you're certainly not as slim as you were when you first came to Windgates.'

'Just as I thought!' Rhoda snapped, her face darkening, 'but need you be so beastly frank about it?'

'I'm sorry,' Jane said a little lamely, 'but I thought you wanted to know.'

Without answering, Rhoda set her lips tightly and drove on in silence, her eyes stormy.

There was more to this plea for reassurance than simple vanity, Jane knew. To this sophisticated woman, her appearance was a matter of vital importance. Her position in life depended upon her being able to present a competent, woman-of-the-world image: it was the image with which she hoped to lure Morris and to show him that, in her, he would have the perfect wife to complement the glossy life he was building up at Windgates.

In an effort to dissipate her tactlessness Jane said, conciliatingly, 'I expect a few days on a diet will do the trick, though, especially if you explain things to Mrs MacInnes. I'm sure she'll understand.'

Rhoda's brow cleared at this peace-offering. 'Yes, you're right. I've always found that I can lose weight if I make up my mind to. It's only a matter of will-power. Well, whether Mrs MacInnes likes it or not I'll simply inform her that I'm not used to a heavy, stodgy Highland diet. It won't do her any harm to have something special prepared for me, for goodness knows the staff is not overworked at Windgates. Morris is not at all fussy about his meals and simply eats whatever's put in front of him. Naturally that spoils the staff. Mrs MacInnes is in clover, catering for a bachelor and getting her own way in everything. She'll find, however, that things will be drastically altered when Morris marries. She won't find life so snug and easy, I can tell you that much. There will be some changes made that she'll find extremely unpleasant.'

So already Rhoda visualised herself as mistress of Windgates, sweeping away the old, easy order of things and instituting a new and much more formal way of life at the old home.

The very contemplation of this new state of affairs seemed to restore Rhoda's spirits, for she said, almost affably, ' By the way, I hear that you were the belle of the ball at the ceilidh. All Kirtleside is ringing with the news. Of course it's only to be expected in a place of this size. But your dress does seem to have created a veritable sensation. Kirstag described it all in detail. According to her the material and colours were quite out of this world—more fit for a state ball than a village ceilidh. What a lucky girl you are to be able to afford such extravagance! I do envy you. Somehow I always seem to be short of money, no matter how I try to economise.'

Jane was completely disarmed by Rhoda's air of affability and impulsively she said, 'Yes, it was very expensive, but I didn't intend to be so extravagant in the first place. My aunt gave me money to buy material—not very much, as you can imagine, for she's not terribly well off, and I was just looking at this cloth in the shop—you know how one does, even though one knows one can't possibly afford it—when who should turn up but Morris. He saw me admiring the material and—'

'Morris! You don't mean to say it was Morris's choice?' Rhoda's voice had risen and her hand jerked on the wheel for an instant so that the car swept out into the middle of the road. But immediately, with her usual competence, she brought it back under control. 'Then what you're really saying is that it was Morris who actually bought it for you?'

Jane was beginning to regret the impulse that had led her to explain the situation concerning the material, but somehow already it seemed too late to draw back.

'Really, Jane, don't you think it was indiscreet, to say the least of it?'

'Yes, I suppose it was,' Jane agreed reluctantly. 'But somehow at the time, it seemed—'

'Seemed? Well, why don't you go on? Seemed what?'

'What I mean is, it didn't appear as unwise as it does now to me, looking back. I suppose it all happened so quickly. It had been bought and parcelled up almost before I knew what had happened. I was looking at the cloth and thinking how wonderful it was and then, suddenly, there he was, and making it all seem so right and so simple that I should take it. Oh, it's hard to explain,' she ended helplessly.

'I'll bet it is,' Rhoda said tightly. 'For heaven's sake, Jane, are you so naïve as to imagine a man gives an expensive gift to a girl without expecting to be paid back somehow or other? Really, to me you sound unnaturally green—or is it just an act on your part?'

'I don't know what you mean,' Jane faltered.

'Don't you?' Rhoda scoffed. 'Oh, for heaven's sake don't be such a fool! Morris is no knight in shining armour, I can assure you, who'll come to the aid of maidens in distress without repayment of any sort. He's a man of the world, and when a woman places herself under an obligation to him, he'll expect repayment. You may be sure of that.'

'Well, yes, I did think of that, of course,' Jane admitted. 'It occurred to me that some time or other I could do some work for him. As you know, I'm an audio-typist and—' She stopped at Rhoda's shrill peal of laughter.

'Really, Jane, sometimes you sound too good to be true! Is this some sort of act on your part? I mean, this terribly ingénue performance you put on. Surely you must realise a man like Morris expects payment of a very different kind?'

'What do you mean?' Jane faltered, although she guessed from Rhoda's manner exactly what she was intimating.

'It's my turn to ask you exactly what you mean,' Rhoda retorted coolly. 'Let's say we take you at your face value and say you actually visualise repaying Morris by stepping into my shoes. How exactly did you imagine such a situation would arise?'

'Well,' Jane considered thoughtfully, 'you might be on holiday, or get a cold, or something.'

'The typical stand-in's dream,' Rhoda retorted acidly. 'Well, for your information, my dear Jane, I've no intention of taking a holiday—at least not now. Why should I? Living at Windgates, as far as I'm concerned, is holiday enough. And as for getting a cold, I'm not given to getting " colds, or something ", so you can put such dreams out of your mind. What you really mean is that you have your eye on my job,' Rhoda pursued furiously. 'You see yourself as stepping into my shoes. Well, no, thanks, I don't need an understudy, so if you're getting ready for the part you're wasting your time!'

'I didn't mean that,' Jane gasped, appalled by the venomous tone in which Rhoda was addressing her.

'Then what did you mean? One thing is very clear, and that is that you're looking forward to the day when I'll no longer be here and you can take my place in Morris's life.'

'That's not true!' Jane cried.

'Isn't it? You're not as naïve as you pretend. You knew perfectly well what you were doing when you accepted that gift from him and knew exactly what obligations you were bringing on yourself.'

She stopped the car abruptly outside the factor's house and Jane got out in silence.

Rhoda leaned her arms on the wheel and surveyed her with eyes full of cold hatred, although her voice was under control. 'Were this to come to your great-aunt's ears it might make things difficult for you. From all I hear she has an almost fanatical hatred of Morris. Suppose she were to discover that you had placed yourself under such an obligation to him, you might no longer be a welcome guest. You might find yourself seated in the next train for London—booted out by your indignant relative.'

With this parting shot she jerked the car into motion and drove off.

Jane felt too disturbed and upset by her conversation with Rhoda to go into the house immediately. She wandered off through the grounds, her mind in a turmoil. What an utter fool she had been to give her confidence to Rhoda! But the secretary had been so pleasant and affable in her manner that she had plunged in without stopping to consider that in Rhoda she had not found a friend, but a bitter antagonist who would furiously resent the smallest intimacy between her and Morris, the man she had earmarked as her own. What if, as Rhoda had hinted, she should choose to make capital of the knowledge she had so unwittingly placed in her hands. Jane shivered a little as she plunged down into the valley. It would mean short shrift for her, as far as Aunt Ellen was concerned, and the first train back to London and her intolerable life with her new stepmother.

Her footsteps unknowingly took her towards the chalets which Morris was having built.

She did not doubt that Ellen would be bitterly disappointed in her, should the truth ever come to her ears. Jane remembered her aunt's pride in the new dress and her assumption that it had been paid for by the small sum she had pressed into Jane's hands before her departure on her shopping expedition.

Her gloomy thoughts were diverted as she came to the end of a narrow tree-shaded path and suddenly found herself before the first of the chalets which was almost ready for habitation. Now she discovered that, overnight it seemed, Morris, with his usual expedition, had had a miniature garden planted, with a tiny lawn and a rockery sloping along the incline to the lower ground. In this, dwarf plants were already blooming and miniature trees stood. She looked at it, delighted at the way the slopes of the ground had been landscaped to make a charming miniature world of flowers and trees and lawn around the newly completed chalet. She was startled at the change in the spot since she had last seen it, but she had to admit to herself that it was quite in keeping with the pace with which Morris got things done that order should replace chaos almost overnight.

Slowly she walked along the narrow path beside the rockery and entered the chalet. It was a single-story bungalow-type of house and she was not surprised to find that it was almost ready for occupation. The walls were unpainted or papered, but apart from that, it seemed complete. The small kitchen was white-tiled and was fitted with the most modern heating and cooking equipment. In the bathroom, she discovered that the electricity was already working so that she was able to switch on and feel the warmth in the towel rails. In the spacious, airy bedroom the wardrobes were built into the walls to give the maximum space. As she stood looking about her, schemes of draperies, colouring and furnishings were becoming clarified in her mind. She felt a sense of excitement as she visualised the rooms as they might appear if she had a free hand with their decoration.

It was the sharp sound of crisp footsteps that aroused her from her daydream. She turned, half-guiltily, to find Morris surveying her frowningly from the doorway.

'And just what are you doing here?' he demanded. 'So you've penetrated the enemy's camp!'

Startled and confused by his sudden appearance, Jane exclaimed, 'Enemy camp? What do you mean?'

'Well, isn't that how you consider me? An enemy?'

'No, of course not! Why should I?'

'Why is it, then, that I get the impression every time we meet that you're continually resisting me? Yes, you can't deny it, Jane. It's as though you were deliberately putting up a barrier as soon as I come on the scene.'

She considered this statement with a solemnity that made him feel exasperated and at the same time amused.

'No, not really,' she said at last. 'It's simply, I suppose, that you're a frightening sort of person, although probably you don't realise that.'

'Me, frightening?' He flung back his head and laughed.

She had not realised until that moment how white and even his teeth were. Nor, for that matter, had she ever heard him laugh so spontaneously, although she couldn't imagine what she had said that appeared to him so amusing.

'Yes, you are!' she reiterated stubbornly. 'You may not realise it, but you are rather overawing.'

'Indeed, then I haven't noticed that I have that effect on Mrs MacInnes or, for that matter, Rhoda.'

Again she considered this statement judiciously. 'Maybe it's because Mrs MacInnes is so much older.'

'I see. And in Rhoda's case, what do you consider accounts for her regrettable lack of awe?'

He was covertly laughing at her, she realised, but somehow it didn't seem to matter and it didn't prevent her from saying gravely, 'I think it's because she's so competent. It must be fun to have such self-confidence, to feel completely in command of the situation.'

' And you, Jane, do you not feel self-confident?'

He had come closer and she was suddenly aware of his nearness. She felt disarmed and vulnerable but determined not to yield. 'No, of course not. Why should I? I've really no particular talents, except,' she ended dryly, ' for daydreaming.'

' And was that what you were doing when I came on you?'

' Well, yes, I was.'

' And what, may I ask, are your daydreams composed of? Knights in shining armour, as usual, I suppose?'

She laughed. ' No, something horribly prosaic, I'm afraid. The decoration of this chalet, in fact.'

He regarded her in silence for a moment and she saw a look of sharp interest in his eyes. ' If your dreams are not too outrageous I'd be glad to get the benefit of them.'

Now that he had asked her, she felt a little shy. 'Well, the bathroom, for instance: I see it in shades of green, aquamarine and jade, to give the effect of water; ivory and pink with touches of mauve in the bedroom, and—' She stopped.

' Yes, go on.'

' Well, for the sitting-room perhaps, as it's big and so well-proportioned, small reproduction pieces would look well there.'

He glanced at her in surprise. ' Reproduction pieces! Well, I must say that's a very different suggestion from Rhoda's: she's all for blond Scandinavian modern furnishings. But now that you mention it, it seems to me an excellent idea.'

Jane led the way into the sitting-room enthusiastically. ' I was thinking a fauteuil here in the corner, perhaps about the period of William the Fourth or early Victorian, before the pieces became too massive, and over here perhaps a small pier table.'

She went on eagerly outlining her suggestions and when at last she drew to a halt, she found that he was regarding her with an expression she found hard to decipher.

' I must say a detailed discussion of the possibilities of reproduction furniture was the last thing I had expected to come from that little head of yours. Tell me, where did you learn to be so knowledgeable about such things? If I remember rightly you told Rhoda you used to be an audio-typist.'

' Yes, but I used to attend a class in interior decoration in the evenings,' she told him.

' I see, so this accounts for the very perspicacious suggestions,' he said slowly. ' Rhoda and I had discussed the interior design of this first chalet. However, neither of us is a qualified designer and you may be sure that I shall listen to your suggestions with great attention. Tell me, Jane, what exactly do you intend to do with your life?'

' I don't know quite what you mean,' Jane said uncomfortably, after a moment.

' What I mean is, how do you visualise your future? Is this interior decorating business to be your interest? Or is there some boy—someone perhaps you've met at evening classes—whom you care for particularly?'

She considered the question. ' No, I don't think there was ever a boy I thought of seriously. I mean, everything was broken up for me when Daddy married again. Somehow it had never really entered my head that he might. I suppose one doesn't. All my dreams came to an end then.'

'But why should that be?'

'I don't think I realised how lonely Daddy was,' she told him thoughtfully. 'Then suddenly somehow Christine was in the house, my new stepmother, and it seemed as if my old life was over for good. Before that I had been selfishly wrapped up in my plans for the future.'

'I see. But why should your father's remarriage have made such a difference?'

When she didn't reply, he said, 'I suppose you don't get along with your father's new wife? That's the usual story, isn't it?'

'No, somehow we didn't see eye to eye,' she admitted.

'And whose fault is it?'

Jane considered. 'I truly don't know,' she said at last. 'I suppose I used to blame Christine. I thought that I'd done everything I could to be friends with her, but now, looking back, I think perhaps I was possessive about Daddy's love. You see, until Christine came on the scene there had only been the two of us and I had always been first with him. Somehow I had childishly thought it would always be like that. But naturally Christine took first place with him; it was only right, of course. After all, she is his wife. I see that now, but at the time I found it hard to adapt myself.'

He regarded her thoughtfully. 'You're growing old beyond your years, my little Jane. Yes, it's true, a man needs a wife, and a young girl can hardly understand that. But the years bring wisdom.'

'Yes, I'm realising more and more that perhaps it would be the best thing for Daddy if I were to stay away.'

'So you won't be going back to London and the life

you had formerly?' he asked. 'All your dreams are at an end? Is that it?'

'Yes, I suppose so,' Jane said reluctantly.

'Then you'll stay with us and make this your home in the future?'

A faint look of surprise crossed his face as Jane shook her head. 'No, I can't stay on here either; not for always: this is just a sort of resting place before I must move on again. You see, Aunt Ellen wants to keep me, but I couldn't possibly sponge on her and make myself a burden on her in her old age.'

'Then what do you intend to do?'

'I don't know exactly,' Jane told him slowly. 'But this holiday with Aunt Ellen is wonderful: it gives me time to think and to try to make plans.'

'Well, take your time deciding on your future. Don't do anything drastic,' he told her. 'Now that we have you here we can't lose sight of you too quickly.'

But would it really matter to him if she were to go away? she wondered a little sadly.

Unconsciously a shade had crossed her face and, as if in answer to that unspoken question, he said softly, 'Yes, even in spite of the fact that you're a stiff-necked, antagonistic, horribly stubborn girl, I don't want to lose track of you, Jane.'

She opened her lips to protest hotly at this unflattering description, but at that moment the door was thrown open and Rhoda entered with her long, swift, graceful strides.

'Oh, Morris, I'm so sorry I'm late,' she began, 'but that interior decorator was on the phone and there was no getting rid of him. He kept yattering on and on and—'

Her words ground to a halt as she caught sight of Jane. 'Oh, hello,' she said. 'You're here.'

'Yes, Jane's here,' Morris told her, a note of dryness in his voice.

Rhoda turned her attention to some papers she held in a big clip-board and when she looked up again her poise was fully restored. 'As I was saying, that interior decorator was on the phone. But whether we should hire him, I really don't know. He has quite a good reputation. On the other hand one doesn't like to take someone completely out of the blue.'

'Somehow I don't think we'll need him after all,' Morris told her.

Rhoda looked at him inquiringly, her fine tawny eyebrows raised. 'No? And why not?'

'Why should we look further afield when we have an excellent decorator on the premises, simply bursting with original ideas?'

As he spoke he turned towards Jane and Rhoda followed his glance, her eyes assuming an expression of wonderment. 'But you surely don't mean Jane?' talent for it. Just listen to the ideas she has suggested.' she asked, a trifle huskily, after a moment.

'Yes, I do indeed,' he told her. 'It seems she has studied designing and, besides that, has an obvious 'Yes, I'm all ears.' Rhoda fixed her eyes on Jane in an attitude of polite inquiry, but Jane could not but be aware of the air of almost palpable irritation and impatience that the secretary was barely keeping within bounds.

'I thought shades of green might be suitable in the bathroom,' Jane began.

'But we've already decided on cream tiles,' Rhoda addressed Morris. 'I thought that was all arranged.'

'But I like the idea of varying shades of green better,' he told her.

Rhoda bit her lip in exasperation and then shrugged. 'Oh, very well. If that's the way you want it. After all, you're the boss. And what are your other brilliant ideas, Jane?' she asked.

'Well, ivory and pink with touches of mauve for the main bedroom,' Jane faltered, under the impact of the secretary's steely air of polite attention.

'And what do you suggest for the sitting-room?'

'Jane thought of reproduction furniture,' Morris put in briskly, 'and I must say I think it's an excellent idea.'

'How charming and olde-worlde!' Rhoda sneered.

'But it's not olde-worlde,' Jane protested defensively. 'It just seems suitable for the chalet and the scenery and the general setting here in Scotland—if you know what I mean. You know what I mean, don't you?' she appealed desperately to Morris.

'Yes, of course,' he replied coolly when Rhoda's short burst of laughter had subsided. 'I may as well tell you now, Rhoda, that I thought of inviting the Mackenzies here as our first guests.'

'Oh! The elderly couple you were telling me of, who were neighbours of yours in Canada?' Rhoda queried.

'The very same! It struck me as Jane was outlining her suggestions that by some sort of magic she had hit upon the exact sort of decor our guests would like and expect in a fishing lodge in Scotland. As she so cleverly suggested, a certain touch of looking backward would be exactly right for the mood.'

A short silence followed this remark.

'I take it then that Swedish furniture with good

clean lines is out. Instead we're to have worm-eaten pieces of ye olde Scotlande, perhaps?'

'Not quite,' he returned quietly. 'By the way, I wish you'd take note of these suggestions and we'll get down to implementing them as soon as possible. Jane could also give us her ideas for the smaller bedroom.'

Together they moved from room to room, Rhoda obediently making notes as Jane threshed out suggestions with Morris.

But as time passed, Jane became more and more uneasy. Granted, Rhoda's manner was now smooth and efficient as usual, but she had darted Jane such a look of malignity that she could not but be aware that under that smooth and faintly smiling mask, the secretary was growing increasingly malevolent.

Matters came to a head as they were leaving.

As they crossed the threshold, Rhoda dropped her clip-board with a resounding crash, the papers spilling into the garden and being carried away a little distance by the soft breeze that was blowing.

While Morris gathered them, Rhoda turned her head towards Jane and in a low, vehement voice said, 'There isn't room for both of us here at Windgates. I'd advise you to leave, before I make things too hot for you!' She would have said more, but at that moment Morris handed her a bundle of papers.

'Oh, thank you, Morris.' Instantly she was the smoothly smiling woman whom he was accustomed to see. 'How stupid of me to drop the board, but I think I've everything here now.'

As the three of them strolled back towards the main house, Jane was thinking that, to any onlooker, they seemed on the best of terms. But Jane could no longer delude herself about the fact that in Rhoda she had a determined and vicious enemy—one who would do her any damage that she could—and she, Jane, had been foolish enough to supply the enraged and jealous woman by her side with a wealth of material by which she could wreck her life.

CHAPTER VII

Some mornings later found Jane standing in the village street waiting for the bus which would carry her into Aberdeen for the day.

Ellen had given her some pocket-money and she had decided to go into town and do a little leisurely shopping. For the trip she had put on one of her remaining good dresses: it was blue, in a linen-finished material, and with it she wore a tiny, stiff white cap which sat jauntily on her brown curls, and white gloves and shoes.

It was a good thing she had remembered to bring a raincoat, she was thinking a moment later, as a heavy summer shower came on. As she unfolded the coat and held it over her head, she looked down disconsolately at her snowy white shoes. A few moments more of this torrential shower and they would be soaked.

It was then that she became aware that a car had stopped just before her and peeping out under the waterproof she saw that it was Morris's and that he was at the wheel.

He threw open the door. 'Do get in,' he urged. 'What on earth are you doing, standing in the street, getting yourself soaked?'

'I'm waiting for the bus,' she told him as she slipped into the car. 'I'm going into Aberdeen to do some shopping.'

'I suppose you're like all women,' he told her. 'No matter how many clothes you have, you feel you "haven't a thing to wear". I like your dress particularly: it's almost the same shade as the blue of your eyes.'

His glance told her that she was looking her best and she felt glad that for once she had met him when she was really well groomed; too often had their encounters taken place when she had been far from tidy. It had been particularly annoying because of the contrast she had presented to Rhoda's invariably trim and poised turn-out.

For a moment or two they sat watching the rain fall in rods and dance and bubble on the bonnet of the car.

He broke the silence with, 'Tell me, Jane, what are you going to do about the furnishing of the chalet?'

'The furnishing of the chalet?' Her voice had risen in surprise. 'But what—what has it got to do with me?'

'I suspected this was your attitude,' he told her a little grimly, 'and I may as well tell you that I'm not going to stand for it.'

'What do you mean?' she asked.

'I mean that I've no intention of permitting you to back out now—not when you've presented me with all sorts of fascinating ideas. Do you mean to say you're hard-hearted enough to do nothing about it?'

Jane was silent for a long moment. Only too clearly could she visualise Rhoda's reaction were she to find that Jane had thrust herself into what the secretary would certainly look upon as her province. 'But isn't Rhoda going to attend to this?' she asked.

'Rhoda?' he inquired. 'Competent as she is, she can hardly be expected to do everything. No, Rhoda has plenty to do taking care of the business side of things.'

'But I don't think she sees it as I do,' Jane faltered.

'What of it?' he retorted. 'I like the way you see it, and that's what matters, isn't it?'

'But—but—' Jane demurred.

'You can't let me down now,' he told her. 'Can't make all sorts of mouth-watering suggestions and then leave me to carry them out as best I can.'

The possibility of being able to choose what she would need to make her dream come true about the chalet was enticing. 'I'd like to—' she began. Then her voice rose. 'Here comes the bus!' She began to scramble from the car.

But he caught her by the wrist. 'What about driving into Aberdeen with me now and you can indicate what you need to carry out your ideas, and whatever isn't to be found there, we'll order by phone from London, or wherever is the best centre.'

'Now?' Jane asked weakly.

'Yes, now. Why not? I don't believe in putting things off once I've made up my mind,' he told her firmly. 'What do you say?'

Dumbly Jane nodded, watching the bus pull out of the village. Things were moving at a faster pace than she had anticipated, she was thinking as the big car slid off towards Aberdeen in the wake of the bus.

The short summer shower was soon over, the sun came out more brilliantly than before, and never had the Highland scenery seemed more beautiful and splendid than it did to her during the drive.

'Order everything you think will be necessary to

make the chalet look as you visualised it,' he told her as they drove into the town.

'But what about prices?' she queried. 'What limit must I keep within?'

'No limit,' he replied. 'After all, this is the realisation of a dream, isn't it? And we mustn't niggle about money where dreams are concerned.'

There followed for Jane a few hours of magic, when she was able to order draperies, upholstery, furnishings and carpets, regardless of cost. It was like having an Aladdin's cave thrown open to her in which she could wander and pick what she wanted to her heart's content. She felt quite dizzy with colours and textures, designs and qualities, when, after she had chosen all she wanted from the stores in the outstanding furnishing shops in the town, Morris put through a call to a famous firm of makers of reproduction pieces in London and told her to order what she desired from their stocks.

When she had done so and was assured that the pieces would be rushed to Kirtleside at the earliest possible moment, she put down the phone and turned to look at Morris with shining eyes.

'Well, do you feel quite worn out?' he asked, smiling.

'I've never had such a wonderful time in my life,' she told him a little breathlessly. 'I didn't know it was possible to have such fun. But—but why are you doing everything in such a rush?'

'There's a story behind that,' he told her. 'Come along. We deserve a spot of lunch after this morning's exertions, and while we eat I'll tell you all about it.'

Soon Jane found herself seated at a table in one of Aberdeen's leading hotels where, to her amusement, he ordered cockaleekie soup and Spey salmon.

'I looked forward to having Scottish food when I decided to come to the Highlands,' he told her. 'You see, that's another way in which we Leslies have kept in touch with the homeland. We used to have Scottish salmon flown in for our big feasts: my grandfather's birthday was such a day! And a real traditional Scottish haggis for Burns's Night.'

Jane looked at him a little wistfully. Now that she was coming down to earth again after her shopping spree, she was very conscious of the amount she had spent at his direction. It must be wonderful to be able to make one's dreams come true regardless of cost.

'Now for the reason for all the rush,' he began with a smile. 'It's because I've invited an elderly couple who were our neighbours when I was a boy to come over for a few weeks' fishing and shooting, and I want to be sure the chalet is ready when they arrive. I owe them a great deal—especially Angus. He took me on my first fishing and hunting trips and taught me how to stand on my own two feet, how to be resourceful and to live off the land. It's to Angus and Flora I owe my love of outdoor life. They helped to give me a wonderful childhood and I could never do enough to repay them.'

As he spoke Jane was toying with her spoon, her thoughts going to her own childhood. There was a pensive look about her lips and he broke off—'But I must be boring you with all this talk about my boyhood! Tell me, what was your childhood like?'

'I was wonderfully happy,' she told him. 'Daddy took me everywhere with him. He took a great interest in historic London. Especially he loved to explore the places in which Dickens' stories were set. We even travelled to Yarmouth and to the White Hart Inn at

Bath. In the Pump Room there I used to be able to imagine Mr Pickwick drinking his glass of sulphur water. Sometimes we went sailing and I soon learned to crew for him. Everything was interesting when I was with him and we had happy times together until—until—'

'Until your stepmother came on the scene, I suppose,' he ended as she faltered to a stop.

'After that nothing was the same,' she agreed.

'So you didn't expect Christine to come on the scene,' he said after a moment. 'Just how did you visualise your future, then?'

'I don't quite know,' she said doubtfully. 'I suppose I thought there would only be Daddy and me until—perhaps until I got married.'

'So you thought your father would wait until Mr Right came along for you! And how did you visualise him, your Prince Charming? What sort of person did you think he would be?'

Jane considered for a moment, her head tilted to one side. 'Someone rather like Daddy, maybe—quiet and easy-going, gentle, good-tempered, not like—' She paused. Not like him, she was thinking; energetic, self-opinionated, dynamic, imperious, wealthy!

'Someone like Gregory Shields, perhaps?' His voice broke into her thoughts.

She glanced at him in surprise, then paused to wonder if he were correct. Was it someone like Gregory Shields she had imagined? Possibly, she told herself doubtfully. Gregory was pleasant, easy-going, unambitious. Even the fact that he was not wealthy but merely comfortably off seemed to fit into that girlish picture of the man in her future. Yet, now that she had met Gregory, she knew that she was not really in love with him.

'You know Gregory Shields is a fine person: he has all the qualities I lack,' Morris told her. 'But if you're looking for someone who is easy-going, then I don't know if he's the right man for you. In fact, in many ways he's not as easy-going as I am myself.'

Jane gave a little trill of laughter as she heard him make this claim.

'I'm quite in earnest,' he assured her. 'I've tried repeatedly to come to terms with him, but he won't make any response to my offers of friendship. He's bitter, resentful, antagonistic. He believes no good of me and spends his time poisoning other people's minds against me. All the overtures of friendship come from me. I'd like to get along with him if I could, but he won't have it.'

As he signalled for the waiter and paid his bill Jane looked at him in surprise. He had put before her a new conception of Gregory, one that cast fresh light upon the feud between the two men.

She was still struggling to adjust her mind to this version of Gregory's character as she went about her personal shopping. She bought shoes of pale green, a summer weight cardigan, stockings and some new underwear, and had her hair shampooed and set. Then she was ready to meet Morris in Union Street for the drive back to Kirtleside.

The afternoon had fled and speedily as the big car had brought them home, the bus was just pulling out as they drove down the village street.

'Better let me off here,' Jane said as she swung around to collect her parcels.

She was startled by his reaction.

'Now don't tell me we're going to go through all this

again!' He sounded exasperated.

'What?' She could feel herself colour.

'Don't pretend to misunderstand me,' he thundered. 'We had exactly the same situation on the last occasion we drove back from Aberdeen. You didn't want me to drive you home then either. Why?'

It was Jane's turn to be annoyed. 'You know perfectly well why!' she said sharply.

'Because your aunt won't suffer you to be in my company! I should have thought you'd have more spunk than to stand for this sort of thing indefinitely. I've a good mind to drive you home whether you like it or not. Ellen Ferguson will have to come to terms with life sooner or later. However, if this is what you want—! It's plain the quiet, unambitious Gregory is the right man for you, so you should take him very seriously,' he told her grimly, as she got out.

She stood regarding him stormily. 'I *do* take him seriously,' she had time to burst out before the car swept away and she was left standing in the village street, her parcels piled in her arms.

As she came abreast of Miss MacKillop's little house, the door opened and Miss MacKillop herself appeared on the doorstep.

'My, so you've been shopping!' she exclaimed. 'I suppose you've just got off the bus. Do come in and have a cup of tea with me. I've a few cakes ready and all they need is a little cream. You promised me you'd call in to taste my cakes, you know, and so far you haven't done so.'

In a few minutes Jane found herself ensconced in a cosy nook in the kitchen. It was clear that already she was being accepted in Kirtleside, she was thinking, remembering that on her last visit she had been relegated to the icy chill of the parlour. Being invited into the kitchen meant that now she was 'one of us'.

As her hostess put the kettle on, Jane leaned back in her chair, feeling suddenly tired. Everything in the kitchen was sparklingly clean: the china shepherdess on the mantelshelf dimpled and smiled in the light from the fire and in every conceivable nook and cranny small objects of brass and copper winked and reflected the room.

As she whipped cream in a bowl, Miss MacKillop chatted. 'Dear me, the new faces we'll have around here soon! Believe you me, in no time you'll be feeling as if you were one of our oldest inhabitants, Miss Talbot. When we have Mr Leslie's friends from Canada—Mackenzie I believe is the name—'

'And my name is Jane,' Jane told her.

'Dear me, is it?' said Miss MacKillop absently. Her attention was engaged in folding cream into a cornucopia of wafer-like pastry. 'And I'm Leah—unusual, but suitable, I'm afraid.'

'Suitable?'

'Yes, it means "weary", you know, and a more wearying job than running a tea-room in the heart of the Highlands I can't imagine. It's not the work, you understand, it's the waiting for customers wears one out. If I didn't have the winter to recover in I don't know what I'd do.'

She said this with such a spry and lively air that Jane had to smile.

'But things are definitely looking up. In no time Kirtleside will be almost cosmopolitan. And when Mr Leslie has all the chalets in operation, why, it will be quite an international centre. But what am I telling you all this for? You're quite in the centre of things there at Windgates and must have all the latest news.'

She darted an inquisitive glance in Jane's direction, and Jane was ashamed to admit that she had heard of the coming of the Mackenzies only that day. Owing to Ellen's feud with Morris the inhabitants of the factor's house received no invitations to Windgates to dinner or to any other event. And while at one time Rhoda used to let drop snippets of gossip, lately she had become sullen and antagonistic in her manner.

'One thing I am delighted about,' said Leah, licking cream from her finger, 'is that Mr Leslie has invited me to the barbecue he's putting on for the people from Canada. I'd have been bitterly disappointed if I'd been left out.'

Again Jane found herself nonplussed. Although she had been in his company all day, Morris had not as much as mentioned to her that a barbecue was mooted.

'That should be very interesting,' she ventured cautiously, 'Barbecues have become so popular in recent times and—'

'Oh, this is not to be *our* kind of barbecue,' Leah informed her, as she reached from the mantelshelf her tea caddy formed in a likeness of Burns's cottage at Ayr. 'This is to be something special. It seems what we look upon as barbecues are only pale shadows of the real thing. In Canada they think nothing of cooking out of doors—the distances are so great, you see. I wonder now if Mr Leslie will preside himself. I shouldn't be the smallest bit surprised if he did, for there's hardly anything he can't turn his hand to. It seems he explored most of Canada before he came back here to the homeland and was able to rough it and survive in the bitter winters they have there. Of course, you can see at a glance he's a man who's used to the great outdoors.'

It was clear from the tone of Leah's voice that Morris could number her amongst his admirers, Jane was thinking, as there was a knock on the outer door and Leah, murmuring, 'Dear me, I wonder who this can be,' disappeared from sight.

Jane, seated in the small kitchen, could clearly hear every word of her conversation with the caller.

'Dr Shields—well, I might have guessed!' Leah was exclaiming. 'There's never a cake or a bun in the house, but you turn up as if by magic.'

'I have a nose for goodies,' Jane could hear Gregory's voice saying as he entered the narrow hall. 'But then it's your own fault, you know. You spoiled me when I was a child, and can't expect me to reform now.'

'So it was the cakes you came for!' Leah's voice sounded arch. 'Or was it perhaps that a little bird told you Miss Talbot was here?'

As she spoke she re-entered the kitchen, followed by the young doctor who, it was plain, felt no surprise at seeing Jane seated there. 'I see you've a nose for cream cakes too,' he greeted her casually.

'So you *did* know she was here!' Leah exclaimed triumphantly as she fetched down from a hook on the dresser a large cup patterned with purple and yellow crocus.

'You've found me out, I see,' he told her. 'Yes, I admit that the grapevine in the village had it that Jane had popped in to see you and I simply couldn't resist—'

'Popping in to see *her*,' finished Leah with a sly twinkle. 'But do sit over to the table. The tea's nicely infused and I want to know what you think of my baking.'

Jane found herself seated opposite Gregory at the well-scrubbed kitchen table, before them a generous selection of luscious cakes, while their hostess poured strong black tea.

'I hope you don't mind breakfast cups,' she glanced momentarily at Jane, 'but I do say there's never a cup of tea as hot and as tasty as the first, so one may as well make it last as long as one can. And talking about cooking,' she turned to Gregory, 'I was just saying to Jane that very probably Mr Leslie will do the roasting of the steaks himself at the barbecue for Mr and Mrs Mackenzie while they're here on their fishing trip.'

'Possibly,' Gregory said stiffly. He seemed absorbed in choosing between an éclair and a giant meringue. 'I've heard of this barbecue. It seems it's to be a real Canadian outdoor sort of feast. It should certainly be interesting.'

'I'm looking forward to it,' Leah told him.

Gregory looked surprised. 'You're going, then?'

'And why not? Mr Leslie called in the other evening and asked me himself.'

'Oh!' said Gregory.

'Yes, "Oh!"' Leah told him tartly. 'But then I suppose you wouldn't go, even if he asked you personally?'

Gregory's glance was reproving. 'You may be perfectly sure I wouldn't go,' he said severely. 'You know my attitude towards Morris Leslie and all he stands for.'

'Well, all I can say is that I wish you'd change your mind,' Leah said energetically. 'I used to think as you do, but that was before I met him. He called in here the other evening and sat there by the fire talking so homely and pleasant. He's trying to be friendly and to fit in and be one of us, and I don't see why we're always keeping him out.'

'So you've been won over by being invited to a tenants' do,' Gregory said severely. 'You know why I think he should be kept out. Look what he's done to Windgates!'

'Yes, but everything he has done hasn't been bad,' persisted Leah. 'Those little houses he's built are going to be as pretty as pictures. If he does up the rest as nicely as he has done the one for the Mackenzies, Windgates will be all the better for it when he's finished. You have to admit that.'

'Well, yes, the chalets are turning out better than I expected; not as much of an eyesore as I'd feared,' Gregory had to admit reluctantly. 'But as for my accepting an invitation from Morris Leslie, it would be sheer hypocrisy for me to go and eat the man's food and partake of his hospitality, feeling as I do about him. Principles are principles, after all, and a man must stick to what is right for him. Not that I'm likely to receive any invitation to a social event at Windgates! Morris Leslie is too well aware of my attitude towards him.'

The discussion had cast a gloom over the cosy tea and as soon as they had thanked Miss MacKillop and praised her cooking sufficiently they went out and Gregory offered Jane a lift home.

As they turned towards Windgates, he asked abruptly, 'Are you attending this barbecue, Jane?'

'No, I haven't been invited,' she told him, unaware of the tone of regret in her voice. 'Anyway, even if I had been, Aunt Ellen wouldn't hear of it.'

'So that's the only reason,' he said, a note of quiet

bitterness in his voice. 'You'd go if you could, wouldn't you?'

Jane considered this for a moment. 'Yes, I suppose I would,' she said thoughtfully. Then impulsively she added, 'Would you not reconsider, Gregory?'

'Reconsider what?' he asked.

'Reconsider your attitude towards Morris. After all, as Leah says, he isn't all bad: he's done a lot of good and—'

'So now you're falling for him too,' he said bitterly. 'No woman seems to be able to resist his charms. In no time those who loathed him when he came here first are singing his praises. Surely you're not going over to his side, Jane?'

'I don't know what to think of him,' she said uncomfortably, after a moment. 'Aunt Ellen hates him so much, and it all seems so unreasonable to me now.'

'Now?' he repeated sharply.

'Yes, at one time I believed everything she told me about him, but—'

'And what made you change your mind?' he asked.

'Well, Aunt Ellen told me that he hadn't paid her enough for Windgates, but when I saw the state of the bedroom I used to sleep in when I came here as a child, I could hardly believe my eyes. It seems that when he bought it, the whole house was in a similar state of disrepair, and if that's so, then it wasn't worth more than he paid Aunt Ellen for it.'

'Whether Morris Leslie paid a fair price or not— and I firmly believe he didn't, otherwise your aunt wouldn't be in such straitened circumstances,' Gregory said grimly, 'one thing is perfectly clear, and that is that you defend him on every occasion. You're in love with him, in fact.'

142

Jane laughed. 'There wouldn't be much use in my being in love with him when he's going to marry Rhoda Mannering.'

'Is that true?'

Jane's heart smote her as she heard the eager tone in his voice. 'I'm quite certain of it,' she replied calmly. 'She's much more to him than just a secretary. He trusts her to take on all sorts of responsibilities outside her ordinary duties. Rhoda's right for him and it can only be a matter of time until they announce their engagement.'

'Well, Rhoda may be right for him, but you're right for me,' he said emphatically. 'We always seem to get along so well, Jane. We understand each other. I'm always so happy in your company—and I believe you enjoy mine. At least I hope so. You like it here at Kirtleside, don't you?'

'Yes, I do,' she replied thoughtfully. 'But Gregory, I can't stay here for ever.'

'And why not?' he asked. 'Why not make up your mind to settle in Kirtleside?'

'For the simple reason that I can't sponge on Aunt Ellen,' she told him. 'She has little enough as it is.'

'But that's not what I intended,' he protested. 'I'm asking you to marry me—that is if you care enough. As for me, I can't get you out of my head. When we're separated I count the minutes until I can see you again. You're the only girl in the world for me, and—'

'Don't, Gregory,' Jane broke in. 'You mustn't think of me too seriously. Remember, I'll probably be going away soon and you'll meet a girl who'll be much more—'

'Never!' he exclaimed. 'I care about you desperately. And as for leaving Kirtleside, I really couldn't bear it. Jane, you simply must say yes.'

'Don't ask me for an answer yet,' she said, troubled.
'I've been here such a short while, I don't really know
you well, and—'

'But you'll think about it, won't you? Maybe in
time you'll grow to care for me just a little—and
believe me, I'd be perfectly content with that.'

'I'll think about it, Gregory,' she told him.

As she got out at the factor's house he leaned from
the window to say earnestly, 'You know, Jane, your
promise to think it over has made me the happiest
man in the world. I'm well aware that you're not in
love with me—not at present, that is—and that's why
I'm well content to wait.'

Aunt Ellen had a visitor, Jane was thinking as she
walked towards the house and dimly discerned two
shadowy figures through the wide picture window of
the sitting-room. Perhaps Kirstag had come to give
Ellen a fitting in her own home. Jane sighed as she
thought that the circle of her great-aunt's acquaintances
was certainly not large. Ellen's forthright and biting
tongue had made her many enemies in the neighbour-
hood and had alienated those who would have been her
friends. There had been much litigation which had
dragged on through the years when she had been mistress of Windgates—bringing enmities that had driven
away from her her more prosperous neighbours who,
if she had been a different type of woman, would have
gathered around her in her declining years.

What was Jane's surprise as she was about to enter
the door to find that the figure that emerged was
Rhoda's.

As Jane looked at her inquiringly, Rhoda paused
and flashed her a triumphant glance. 'Don't linger

on the doorstep,' she said, mocking, 'unless you're afraid to go in! Your great-aunt has something to say that should be of great interest to you.'

With these mysterious words she turned away with her graceful, swinging stride along the path in the direction of the main house.

'You traitor!' was the epithet with which Ellen greeted Jane as she entered the sitting-room. Jane looked at her in alarm. The old lady was deathly pale and her eyes were flashing with rage and indignation. 'To think that you, my own flesh and blood, could do this to me! Oh, I didn't think you were capable of it, Jane.'

'But what's—what's wrong?' Jane whispered, appalled at the change that had come over her great-aunt.

This was no longer the relation who had treated her with unvarying kindness and consideration, who had given her shelter and protection when her step-mother's unkindness had driven her from the home which had once been hers. Now Ellen faced her with a look of terrible anger and condemnation.

'Don't stand there and pretend you don't know what I'm talking about,' she cried. 'You let me think your dress was bought with the money I gave you, together with a little of your own—instead it was paid for by Morris Leslie, that robber, that beast, that cruel, revengeful man, who has robbed me of my home and left me to eke out the last years of my life in penury, a pensioner on his bounty on the very lands that are mine by right!'

So Rhoda had at last carried her threat into action, Jane was thinking dully. She had gone to Ellen with the story which Jane had so foolishly revealed to her, of the truth concerning that wonderful dress that she had worn at the ceilidh. Rhoda had taken her revenge for the friendship Morris had shown her by trying to turn Ellen against her.

'How you could have stooped to beg and cringe and take a miserable bit of fabric from that man is more than I can understand,' Ellen was saying. 'But then perhaps I don't understand what it is to be a pretty girl and to feel that one must be the belle of the ball, no matter how one sinks one's pride,' she added with bitter contempt.

Jane stood before her tongue-tied, almost as pale as Ellen herself. It had come at last, something she had dreaded, and now it had burst upon her so unexpectedly. In a moment or two Ellen would pronounce the words of doom. She would order her to pack her few possessions and return to the home of her stepmother. Jane could feel herself tremble and shrink, waiting for this final blow.

'Do you deny that you accepted this present from Morris Leslie?' Ellen demanded. 'Let me hear the truth from your own lips—maybe that Mannering woman has been telling me a pack of lies. I wish I could believe that.'

Jane licked her dry lips. 'She's told you the truth,' she said in a small voice.

There was a long pause while Ellen looked at her fixedly, her face full of sorrow. 'Well, at least you've owned up, and that's something,' she said at last. 'But I still don't know how it could have happened.'

'I don't know quite how it happened myself,' Jane told her. 'I was looking at the fabric—just admiring it, you understand, when suddenly he came up behind me. It was he who ordered the assistant to parcel it up, and somehow I found myself outside in the street, and it seemed that there could be no returning it.'

Ellen's stern face softened slightly as she listened to this confused explanation. 'I think I know how it was,' she said after a moment. 'I know something of what a bully and a tyrant that man is. It must have been difficult for a young girl to stand up to him. Oh yes, I think I know something of the arrogant, ruthless, proud nature of Morris Leslie. And for that matter, I think I know something of the nature of that woman of his, that Rhoda, who went to so much trouble to make sure the story came to my ears.'

Jane waited, her breath held. What was Ellen about to say? Her whole future hung on the old lady's next words.

'I'm glad she told me—make no mistake about that, Jane,' Ellen went on. 'But I'm under no illusion about her motives. She's infatuated with Morris Leslie and she was hoping I would send you away—you, my last living relative. But she must take me for a bigger fool than I am. Well, I won't drive you away. I wouldn't please Miss Rhoda Mannering to do it, even if I weren't fond of you, Jane. I won't let you go, but I must have your word that such a thing will never happen again.'

It was easy for Jane to give this promise, for the business of accepting the fabric was something she was not at all proud of. Looking back, she wondered how she could ever have placed herself in such a position. 'You may be sure that next time I won't let Morris Leslie talk me into doing anything I don't want to do,' she assured Ellen.

'It may not be as easy as you think,' Ellen told her. 'For the man's ways are not our ways. All this modern hustle and push is not at all like the life we're accustomed to in Kirtleside.'

Ellen regarded Jane earnestly. 'I only hope that what you're saying means that you're not in love with him,' she went on in a troubled manner. 'That is the only thing I should dread.'

'In love with him!' Vehemently Jane denied it even while her heart told her that she was not being honest. 'Everyone thinks I'm in love with Morris, but it's not true.' If she did love him did that mean she must not wear her heart on her sleeve?

'Everyone says so?' Ellen queried. 'Does everyone include Gregory? Now there's a man who is truly in love with you. He would propose if you would give him the smallest encouragement.'

As Jane was silent Ellen, with unusual perspicacity, added, 'Perhaps he has already asked you.'

As Jane nodded, Ellen asked eagerly, 'And did you say yes?'

'I couldn't—' Jane began.

'And why not?' Ellen interrupted fiercely.

'I promised him I'd think it over,' Jane told her miserably.

'You must accept him,' Ellen urged. 'Give me your word you'll say yes. Promise!'

'I can't promise,' Jane protested, although her heart smote her for the grief in the old lady's face. 'But I'll think it over.'

As she spoke she was alarmed by the change that came over Ellen. She sank back in her chair with a look of exhaustion in her face, which had become frighteningly pale.

'Aunt Ellen!' Jane sprang to her side. 'Let me help you to bed. You look so ill.'

When she had tucked Ellen into bed and had given her a hot drink, Jane returned to the sitting-room. For a while she stood looking out over the valley where now the wound made by the cutting of so many trees was beginning to heal owing to the pretty patch of garden where the Mackenzies' chalet nestled.

It was Rhoda's ruthless, possessive infatuation for Morris which had brought this suffering upon Ellen, she was thinking bitterly. Rhoda had determined to get her revenge for the interest and pleasure Morris had shown in her suggestions for the chalet—but the blow had fallen not upon her, but upon Ellen.

With a sigh Jane stooped to pick up her parcels. How she had enjoyed her time with him in Aberdeen that day, she was thinking wistfully. But there must be no more such occasions. Should they come to Rhoda's ears there was no knowing what she might do and it was plain that as long as she got her way, Rhoda did not care who suffered.

CHAPTER VIII

On the following morning, Ellen stayed in bed, and when Jane went in to see her, she was alarmed at how pale and fatigued her great-aunt looked. 'Perhaps I should ring for Gregory,' she said anxiously. 'I'm very worried about you.'

'Nonsense, child,' Ellen said firmly. 'There's nothing wrong with me but idleness. I like lying in bed and having my meals brought in to me. I'll be up and around in no time.'

But days passed and although Ellen got up and pottered in the garden once more, she still did not seem to Jane to be completely recovered.

However, Ellen only showed irritation when her great-niece tried to persuade her to rest. 'Do go off for a walk, Jane. It will freshen you up,' Ellen told her with more than a hint of exasperation. 'I never could stand being coddled and don't intend to begin now. You've been so much in the house lately that you're beginning to look pale and wan yourself.'

Obediently, Jane strolled into the village, but when she had called in to Kirstad, had had a chat with Leah MacKillop, and had bought stamps at the post-office, there was nothing more to do, and she turned back towards Windgates in a leisurely way.

As she went along the avenue she caught a glimpse of the roof of what everyone now referred to as 'the Mackenzie chalet', and to her surprise she thought she saw a wisp of smoke. She stopped and stared, shading her eyes against the sun. Yes, there was definitely a thin trickle of smoke above the roof of the little house. She gave a gasp of alarm and was about to run towards Windgates with the news that the chalet must be on fire, when Morris's voice said at her shoulder,

'Don't be alarmed; the chalet's not on fire. What you see is smoke coming from the chimney I've had built into the sitting-room. I thought it would be in keeping with the decor you suggested.'

Jane turned to look at him, unaware that there was a faint expression of reproach on her face.

He raised his hand in a placatory gesture. 'All right, all right. So I did wrong not to consult you! But really, Jane, you're such a cantankerous, bad-tempered, impossible sort of girl that I haven't been able to pluck up courage to approach you!'

What he meant was that he had not forgiven her

for the clash of wills that had occurred at the end of their last visit to Aberdeen, she was thinking.

' But rightly or wrongly, the chalet's ready, and I've incorporated nearly all your ideas. I admit I've had one or two changes made, such as the installation of the chimney in the sitting-room, but I hope you'll approve. The Mackenzies are due to arrive in a few days and the more I see of it the more I believe that your slightly backward-looking decor is going to delight them. Their home is full of lovely old pieces, and this means that coming here will not be too abrupt a change from their own way of life. They're a wonderful old couple, Jane. You're going to like them, I know—just as they're going to like you.'

' I hope they'll like it,' she said, smiling shyly, delighted with his praise.

' You " hope they'll like it ",' he mimicked her prim tones. ' Is that all you have to say? If they're happy here and their visit is a success it will largely be due to you.'

There flickered through Jane's mind the thought that it was a pity that Ellen was on such bad terms with Morris—and, as a consequence, with his guests. It would have been so pleasant to have been able to meet the Mackenzies on easy friendly terms and perhaps to hear from their own lips their comments on what had been done to the interior of the chalet. But this could never be.

Unconsciously she gave vent to a sigh.

' Why so mournful, Jane?' he teased.

' Oh, I was just thinking that the Mackenzies sound a very nice couple,' she told him evasively. ' I'd like to have seen the interior of the chalet now that it's finished—to see how it worked out.'

'You shall certainly see it—and right away. Why not come down with me now? As a matter of fact I've been wondering if I might have your words of wisdom concerning the final touches.'

Together they moved along the path leading down into the valley. Suddenly Jane stopped. Were Rhoda to come upon them alone in the chalet she would undoubtedly report it to Ellen, and Jane shrank from the possible consequences.

'I—I— Not today,' she stammered.

He regarded her, his friendly expression changing to one of hard resentment. 'Very well, if you'd rather not. I suppose you've grown weary of the subject and have lost interest in it.'

'No, of course not! But some—some other time, when—'

'When you're not so busy, perhaps,' he ended. 'Don't worry, I've got the message. You're indifferent, and don't mind if I know it.' As he spoke he turned away and with a little dismissing wave of his hand plunged down the path and was lost to view behind a clump of trees.

As Jane returned to the avenue and slowly continued her walk back to the factor's house, she was thinking bitterly that, torn between her love for Morris and her affection for Ellen and her sense of duty towards her, there seemed to be no solution to the problems that beset her.

After that, Jane saw Morris only at a distance. The Mackenzies arrived and although they had dinner every evening at Windgates and many social occasions were organised for them at which Rhoda played the part of hostess for Morris, Ellen and her great-niece were, of course, never invited.

Their information about the interesting happenings at Windgates came to them through Maggie who loved to regale them with the latest news in a triumphant sort of way, implying—and *you* weren't invited—so *there*!

On the morning of the day the long-awaited barbecue was to be held, she clapped down plates of porridge before them, saying, 'You'll no be going to the barbecue, I fancy.'

Ellen put down the milk jug with an exasperated little crash. 'You may be perfectly sure we're not going to the barbecue! You've lived all your life in Kirtleside, Maggie, and you should know better than to ask such a question.'

'It was just,' said Maggie with deceptive sincerity, 'that I've been invited and I wanted to make sure you have everything for the evening.'

'We'll manage quite nicely, thank you, while you attend this social event,' Ellen told her haughtily. 'And if you feel fatigued in the morning, you needn't come in. It takes place quite late in the evening, if all I hear is correct.'

'Oh aye, it's to be after dark,' Maggie acceded, 'but it'll be all the more fun for that, you may be sure. There's many a nice shady nook there along by the river where a lad might kiss his lassie coming through the rye, if you know what I mean.'

'No, I don't know what you mean,' Ellen said severely. 'It's "a' the lads they *smile* at me when coming through the rye"—or was, when I was a girl—although times have changed, no doubt.'

The old lady spoke with every sign of irritation, but Jane had long ceased to worry about her great-aunt's tussles with the irrepressible Maggie Crampsie. She had remonstrated with Maggie at first and had secretly asked her to be more deferential in her behaviour, but Maggie had answered, ' Heaven help us, the poor body enjoys every word of it. Crossing swords with me is a sort of comfort to her in her old age.'

Gradually Jane had come to the conclusion that there was a great deal of truth in this. Ellen seemed the better and spryer on a morning when she had had a good passage of arms with Maggie from which she had emerged victorious—or so she thought, for Jane had come to realise that on many occasions Maggie adroitly gave her the last word.

' They tell me everyone is welcome at this outdoor feast, but I can assure you that everyone is not there as long as the Fergusons don't attend. Our absence will be noted, you may be sure of that, and commented upon, and people will wonder why. Oh, Mr Morris Leslie can't pull the wool over everyone's eyes in spite of all his money, you may be sure of that.'

' Oh aye, he'll be real sorry the Fergusons arenae there, no doubt,' returned Maggie with a knowing wink in Jane's direction.

Jane pretended not to see this, but she couldn't help feeling that Maggie by her wink had shown that she assessed Morris's probable reaction very accurately. No doubt he would note the absence of the people from the factor's house, but he would hardly worry about it.

It did not seem to have struck Ellen that they had not been invited.

It was true it was general knowledge that he was holding open house and that everyone at Kirtleside was welcome, but he had also gone to the trouble of asking certain people especially; Leah, for instance, and Kirstad too, as Jane had discovered. But they had received no invitation.

After breakfast Jane strolled out into the grounds and went as far as a rustic white-painted seat set in a grove of young trees from which one could look down over the valley to the river. From this spot the preparations which had been made for the numbers whom Morris expected to attend the barbecue were evident. The paths beside the river had been widened and lights had been strung through the trees.

Life was so complicated, she was thinking, as she sank upon the rustic seat and propping her chin on her clenched fist gave herself up to the problems that loomed so large on the horizon of her life.

There was the question of what she was to do about Gregory's proposal. They had met several times and while he had shown her in a multitude of ways that he looked upon her as the only girl in his life, yet, true to his promise to give her plenty of time, he had not urged her to give him an answer. However, he would not wait for ever, she knew. Nor did she wish to put him off too long. He was too fine a person to have his feelings trifled with and a refusal after a long time when perhaps he had come to believe that an acceptance was inevitable, would be a blow to his pride—and would be a miserable repayment for the friendship he had shown her.

' Tell me, what are you thinking about so earnestly?'

She turned her head to find that Morris had seated himself on the bench beside her.

' But then you're an earnest sort of person, aren't you, Jane, or is it just that you're so young—somehow the young always seem so much more sincere and care-worn than us elderly persons.'

He was smiling as he spoke and Jane thought she

had never seen him look so full of life and energy.

He had spoken lightly, but she was aware that there was something different in his attitude towards her and was quite bowled over when he said, 'I've come to apologise, Jane.'

'What?'

Her voice had risen in surprise and he smiled wryly as he said, 'Your amazement only confirms my own conclusion that this is long overdue. If an apology from me is such an astonishing thing then it's high time I mended my ways.'

'But what have you to apologise for?' she asked, bewildered.

'A great deal, I'm afraid,' he returned. 'Do you remember saying to me one day—it was when we were looking at the chalet together, I think—that I'm a frightening sort of person? I laughed at the time, but I've taken it to heart since then and I want to remedy that.'

'But why?'

'Do you really not know why?'

She shook her head.

'Because there must be something far wrong when you won't have anything more to do with me.'

She looked at him in surprise, but he was gazing across the vista down the valley and did not return her glance.

'You've completely altered your attitude towards me in recent weeks. When we went over the chalet together and discussed it, you were all enthusiasm and I believed then that while no doubt you did it because it was fun, yet also you liked me a little and wanted to help.'

She nodded and he continued, 'Yet when it came to

viewing your handiwork, in the flesh so to speak, you wouldn't please me even to look at it. Isn't that so?'

' No,' Jane protested. ' No, it wasn't—'

' You wanted to see how the chalet had turned out: you can't deny that, Jane. You were even walking towards it when something struck you and you drew back. Your refusal was a personal matter—personal in connection with me—that's all I can assume. You were showing me you disliked me too much to take an interest in what concerns me. Or perhaps it would be nearer the truth to say you were showing me you didn't intend to put up any longer with my bad manners and that you were going to hold out until you received an abject apology. You know, sometimes you seem so young that I think of you as a child, but you're woman enough to wish to bring a man to heel, and if an apology is what you want then you shall have it. I apologise—abjectly. There!'

Jane could hardly forbear smiling at this idea of an abject apology. Instead, she said very gravely, ' I accept it if you insist, although what it's for, I don't quite know.'

' That doesn't matter!' He brushed aside her objection. ' The important thing is that you were annoyed with me and now you're satisfied. And now that that's settled, I want you to come to the barbecue this evening. And this time there must be no refusals!'

Jane gasped at this unexpected change of subject.

'The great majority of people in Kirtleside will be there. Why should you and your great-aunt be the exceptions? Not, of course, that I'm foolish enough to hope that she will come! But you're a different matter. Were you to refuse I should be seriously hurt.'

He was making it as difficult as possible for her to

say no, she knew, but she had been touched by the sincerity under his abrupt and cavalier apology, and knew that it had not been just a preliminary to this demand.

How she wished she dared accept!

It would have been fun to mingle with the crowd that would be there; to meet her neighbours and chat in a carefree manner; to laugh and joke with young people of her own age, away from the melancholy and lonely life at the factor's house. Especially it would have been nice to meet the Mackenzies—to hear perhaps their words of praise for the manner in which the chalet had been prepared for them.

She said this to him.

'There's nothing I should like better,' she told him sadly. 'It would have been wonderful—such fun! Everyone in Kirtleside is looking forward to it. It would have been nice to meet Mr and Mrs Mackenzie and to hear what they think of the chalet.'

'You sound as if you're refusing, Jane,' he said slowly. 'But why? If you sincerely wish to meet the Mackenzies why should you not do so? They're anxious to meet you, I can tell you that. Their holiday is drawing to a close. They seem to have enjoyed themselves and you must let them thank you for your contribution to their happiness.'

'I can't go, Morris!' Her refusal was almost a wail.

'Why not?' he demanded.

As she did not reply, he went on grimly after a moment, 'Because of your great-aunt, of course! She hates me with an undying hatred. You'd think I was her worst enemy. But you know better than that, don't you, Jane?'

She was touched to hear the appeal in his voice.

Very few must have heard those accents from this tough, self-confident man.

'I know she has spread the story—and to give her her due I believe she's convinced of it herself—that I robbed her when I bought Windgates. But the truth is she can't forget that I'm a descendant of the Leslies who were dispossessed in the days of the clearances. She sees it as revenge on my part, but you don't believe it, do you, Jane?'

'I did at one time,' she admitted, 'but when I saw the condition of the room that used to be mine when I came here as a child, I realised that you had given a fair price.'

'Well then, what further difficulties are there? If that's your attitude there's no reason why you shouldn't join us this evening.'

'It's not as simple as that,' she protested. 'Aunt Ellen gets so terribly upset when she thinks I'm friendly with you. She thinks I'm betraying her and—'

'And going over to the enemy, isn't that it? You must know what nonsense that is, Jane.'

'Yes, but remember I'm staying with her as her guest. I simply can't upset her and go against her wishes and—'

'Come, Jane,' he interposed. 'You're not a child any longer. Your aunt's attitude does no one any good —neither you nor herself. Why don't you take your courage in both hands and simply tell her that you're coming?'

'I couldn't do such a thing,' she protested. 'I owe a loyalty to her.'

'And you owe some fairness to me,' he urged. 'I'm heartily sick of being in the doghouse. I feel things too, you know. Believe me, I may pass it off as a joke, but it pains me to be treated as an outcast here in Kirtleside. I've done my best to get along with the people here and I've succeeded in making many of them my friends. But I'm ostracised by others. Gregory Shields hates me, and I can guess why—at least I can guess at the motive for his recent dislike of me—and I must say that there he has my sympathy.'

'Now what do you mean by that?' she asked.

'I mean that you're a bone of contention between us, Jane. Gregory likes you too much for his own good, while I—'

'Yes?' She waited, her breath held.

But abruptly he reverted to his original subject. 'All I can say is that Gregory won't respond to any overtures I make to him. And while, as I say, to a certain extent I can sympathise, yet I'm heartily sick of it. You must be fair to me, Jane.'

'I—I am fair to you, Morris,' she told him almost timidly.

'Then show it by nailing your colours to the mast and coming to the barbecue.'

'But I can't,' she cried.

'Very well!' He rose to his feet. 'A man can take only so much. He can beg and plead with a woman, but not for ever—at least I can't. I'm not that type of man. I've done everything I can think of to make you change your attitude towards me, but if I've failed —well then, that's just too bad. Make up your mind what you're going to do, because I shall never plead with you again.'

As she watched his broad-shouldered, strong figure move away, Jane was thinking—

If only I could tell you that the woman you love will not permit us to be in each other's company, even for a little while. I dare not show you the friendship I feel for you because I'm afraid she would take it out on someone who is old and frail, and whom I love dearly in spite of her faults and her wilful antagonism towards you!

That evening Ellen went off to bed early. She had been drowsing over her knitting and eventually she rolled up the sleeve of her latest jumper and put it into the raffia bag with the blue roses on it and saying goodnight with a yawn went away to her room.

Jane remained in the sitting-room for a while, gazing out disconsolately over the twilight-filled valley in which already she could make out the gleams of the fairy lights strung up through the trees along the river bank. She could hear cars drive up to the main house and the distant slam of a door as guests got out and began to wander down through the paths beside the chalets towards the grassy patch beside the river where the barbecue was set out.

She stood disconsolately by the wide picture window for a while, then slowly turned towards her room. She closed the door behind her and sank down on her bed, her mind in a turmoil of indecision.

Morris would think it so strange if she didn't turn up. Would he despise her for cowardice? she wondered, as she remembered how he had urged her to stand up to Aunt Ellen. It was easy for him, she thought a little resentfully. He was his own master, able to make decisions as he wished, but her life was complicated by the fact that she was Ellen's guest. She had made one or two attempts to pluck up her courage, but had not been able to bring herself to ask Ellen if she might go.

She would just go to bed, she told herself. But

never had she felt more wide awake. Her bedroom seemed poky and oppressively stuffy. She moved about restlessly. What would Morris think when he found she hadn't put in an appearance? It was clear that his patience was nearly at an end. Her anxiety to please Ellen seemed to him to be no more than a craven submission to the dictates of a tyrannical old woman. Jane shrank from telling him that Rhoda had visited Ellen personally to make sure she heard that her great-niece had accepted a gift from the enemy. Even if she were to steel herself to make such a complaint would it be possible for him to understand Ellen's reaction to the news—her shame and bitter sense of betrayal that one of her blood should have put herself under such an obligation.

There was also the thought of the Mackenzies to add salt to the wound: they would perhaps be ready to thank her and to discuss the furnishings and decoration of their chalet.

Gradually Jane became more and more resentful of the fate that held her prisoner here in the house when there seemed no reason why she shouldn't attend.

Finally, after another half hour of indecision, her mind was made up: she would slip out to the barbecue for a little while. Having put in an appearance she would then be able to leave early. Ellen need never be the wiser.

Silently she stole from the house, her breath catching in her throat as the door slipped into place with a little slam that reverberated in the twilight air. She hesitated for a moment, then turned away and was running on silent feet towards that place of light and gaiety by the river bank.

Here she recognised people whom she knew lived

in the district but whom she had never met or spoken to because of Ellen's feuds with her neighbours. What a pity the old lady had cut herself off from those who would gladly have shown her friendship, Jane was thinking, as she mingled with the strolling crowd.

Soon she caught sight of Rhoda dressed in snowy shorts and dark tee shirt: around her slender throat a tawny tinker scarf a tone darker than the shade of her hair which was hanging down her back and tied with a huge white bow. In this informal attire Rhoda seemed younger and very happy as she greeted Morris's guests. And suddenly Jane saw that at this gathering Rhoda was acting as his hostess and that she was revelling in her part—obviously seeing this as only one of many such occasions.

There was surprise in her expression as she caught sight of Jane. 'Oh, so you managed to come!' she said ungraciously. 'Tell me, did your great-aunt give you permission to mix with the no-class people who now inhabit Windgates—or did you by any chance sneak out unbeknownst? Morris didn't seem to know whether you'd be able to get away or not.'

'No, she didn't know whether her strict guardian would permit her to come out as late as this.'

Jane turned to find that Morris was speaking. With him were a snowy-haired man and woman whom she instantly guessed to be the Mackenzies.

'I—I just slipped out for a little while. I shan't be staying long,' Jane stammered. Then her attention was diverted as Morris introduced her to the Mackenzies.

'So this is the clever girl who made it so comfortable for us,' boomed Angus Mackenzie.

'We were entranced when we saw it,' Flora Mackenzie put in. 'It was all so beautifully thought out. I suppose you don't mind if we copy a few of your ideas when we get back home.'

Jane felt a thrill of pleasure at the warmth of their praise of her handiwork.

While she had been speaking to the Mackenzies, Morris had wandered off to join Rhoda, who was now supervising at the barbecue, her face faintly flushed as she roasted steaks over the glowing charcoal. Meanwhile Morris was stirring something in a large, heavy pot.

'Um, I think I recognise the scent of that sauce,' Angus murmured after a little while. 'Morris was always a dab hand at a barbecue.'

They moved towards where the crowd was now assembled around the charcoal grill and Angus greeted Morris, 'Smells good.'

'I haven't lost the touch yet,' Morris told him. 'It's strong enough anyway: I've given it plenty of chilli and spices.'

'Reminds me of the old days when we used to go on hunting and fishing trips,' Angus said. 'You were only a lad then, but already you could dish a mouth-watering sauce.'

'I miss those trips,' Morris told him. 'I enjoyed myself so much and—'

Just then Rhoda turned to Morris. 'These steaks are nearly ready,' she told him. 'How is the sauce coming along?'

'Just about right,' he replied, 'but I'd give it a moment or two longer.'

Angus tapped him on the shoulder. 'Leave it in the capable hands of this young lady.' As he spoke he glanced towards Jane with a smile. 'There's something I must discuss with you before we leave and we'll probably be rushing for the plane in the morning and forget all about it.'

'Here, I think this is ready now,' Morris told Jane, handing her the pot. 'Just put a dollop on each plate. You'll be able to manage, won't you?'

As Jane took the pot from him the heavy dark liquid was bubbling. 'Careful now: the handle's hot,' he warned. As he spoke he wrapped a thick cloth about the handle and now she was able to manage it much better.

He strolled away with Angus while Rhoda put the first steak on a plate and held it out for Jane to add the sauce. She did this carefully, then gradually gained confidence as in rapid succession plates piled with steaks, sausages, and chicken were held before her and she added the sauce before they were borne away by willing hands. As the sauce went off the boil and ceased to bubble she found it more easy to handle the large, heavy pot.

After a while Morris strolled back with Angus and called out to Rhoda, 'Well, how are things going?'

She turned her head to answer him. 'Fine! Everyone's crazy about your sauce.'

'Come, you must let me have some of that,' Angus said. 'I'm the proper person to pronounce the final word. I'm a connoisseur when it comes to barbecue sauces.'

'You shall certainly have some,' Rhoda laughed. As she spoke she placed a tender steak upon a plate and, without turning her head, thrust it towards Jane. The plate struck against the handle of the heavy pot, and in a trice it had swung around under the cloth and the hot liquid had poured over the fingers of Rhoda's right hand.

'Oh!' She snatched back her hand with a gasp, the plate falling to the grass with a dull thud. Then as she felt the pain of the burn she caught up the fingers of her right hand with her left. 'You did that deliberately!' she cried in a clear carrying voice that must have been heard by all those around.

'It was an accident,' Jane protested, appalled.

'Hurry, Jane, ring Gregory Shields and ask him to come to the house.' Suddenly Morris had taken command of the situation.

As he moved towards Rhoda, Jane turned and ran towards the house along the pathways that had become so familiar to her during her walks about the grounds. She dashed across the hall, burst into the library and feverishly dialled Gregory's number, only to get the engaged signal. Again and again she tried, the minutes passing which seemed hours to her in her state of anxiety. But eventually she got through to him and gave the message, as Morris came in supporting Rhoda.

'Well, is he coming?' Morris demanded as he laid Rhoda in one of the deep armchairs and raised her feet upon a stool.

'Yes, I got through in the end,' she told him. 'His phone was engaged at first, but eventually—'

'You told him what had happened?' he demanded, his manner so brusque as to be downright rude.

They waited in silence, Morris pacing up and down the library, his eyes going to the door every few moments as if by magic Gregory could appear already. 'If only I'd stayed and served the sauce myself!' he exclaimed after a few moments.

So he blamed her for what had happened, Jane was thinking. But this was no time to defend herself. Silently she prayed that the burn might not be too severe, but the sight of Rhoda's pain-twisted face and the sound of the low groans that were forced from her lips made her realise how the other girl was suffering.

By the time Gregory arrived Rhoda was sobbing wildly, her hair was streaming over her shoulders and her face was tear-stained. Never had Jane seen her look as she did then: her sophistication had quite vanished and a pain-ridden, frightened girl had appeared. Morris's face was grim and drawn and it was plain that he was deeply affected.

'Well, that must be pretty painful, but it's not as bad as I feared,' Gregory said cheerfully as he examined the hand. 'The sauce can't have been boiling when this happened?' he remarked to Jane.

'No, it had cooled a bit,' Jane began. 'You see—'

'It was boiling!' Rhoda cried out in a wild voice. She burst into loud sobs. 'Can't you give me something to ease the pain?' she wailed.

For an instant Gregory regarded her, then said quietly, 'I don't doubt that the burn is painful and you're frightened and have had a bad shock. I'll give you something to soothe you.'

When the hand was bound up and Rhoda had swallowed the tablets he gave her, Gregory said to her, 'You may as well get off to bed now. And you could rest tomorrow. I'll come in and have a look at your hand.' He glanced at Jane. 'You look a bit shot-up yourself, Jane. Better get off home as soon as you can.'

As he went out, Rhoda sank back upon her cushions with a groan and closed her eyes, and Morris bent and lifted her up carefully and carried her out of the room, while Jane stared after him guiltily.

He had said hardly anything to her since the accident had happened, but it seemed clear that he blamed her for causing such suffering to the woman he loved.

For a moment she had a cowardly longing to flee from the house before he came downstairs again. She would be better able to meet his rancour in the morning. But some stubborn streak in her character made her stay on.

When he re-entered the library, he said abruptly, 'Well, Mrs MacInnes is with her now and in a few minutes she'll be asleep, I hope.' He went over to the fireplace and gazed down into the flames with a troubled face.

Still he hadn't said whether he blamed her or not, Jane thought, waiting timidly.

She drew in her breath with a little gasp of horror, as he raised his head and looked at her, his face full of anger. But, to her relief, she discovered that it was not directed at her. 'That fellow, how callous he is!' he exclaimed. 'Pretending that the burn was nothing! Why, when I gave the pot to you the sauce was boiling!'

Would it comfort him to know the sauce had cooled considerably by the time it touched Rhoda's fingers, Jane wondered, or would he merely think that she too was unfeeling?

'You don't—don't believe what Rhoda said—about my deliberately burning her?' she began a little breathlessly.

'No, of course not,' he said a little irritably. 'She was shocked and in great pain. What a fantastic idea! People don't know what they're saying at such times. Do be a sensible girl, Jane, and don't give it another thought.'

Her relief was so terrible at this reassurance that she could almost feel her knees buckle under her. Suddenly she felt overwhelmingly tired.

'Come to think of it, you look like a girl who could do with being tucked up in her bed,' Morris told her. 'I'll drive you home, and no demurs, if you please. Your great-aunt will be asleep by this time. You can renew your assaults on me in the morning—but for heaven's sake let's have a truce for a few hours.'

'Yes, Morris,' she said meekly as she followed him across the hall. She got into the car beside him and in a few moments was being whirled towards the factor's house.

CHAPTER IX

On the following morning as they made a leisurely breakfast Maggie came in with an envelope. 'For you!' she announced, handing it to Jane.

Jane was astonished to find that it contained a note from Morris in which he asked her to come across to the house to do some typing.

'There must be something extraordinary in that letter,' Ellen told her dryly. 'Your eyes are as round as saucers—and almost as large.'

Jane hesitated an instant, then placed the letter in her hand. Ellen would have to know some time, and it would be as well to get it over with, as soon as possible.

Her reaction was just as Jane expected. She flung down her napkin on the table in an angry gesture. 'So Mr Morris Leslie would like you to attend at Windgates to do some typing while his secretary is laid up! Such cheek! Well, you can send him a reply immediately, Jane, and let him know here and now that no one of my flesh and blood will do any favours for him.'

'But this is not a favour, Aunt Ellen,' Jane told her when the old lady had finally emptied the vials of her wrath and had completely run out of words.

'What's that?' Ellen looked nonplussed. 'Just give me one good reason why you should rush off to do that man's bidding!'

'You know the reason very well, Aunt Ellen,' Jane told her. 'Remember how angry you were about my accepting the dress fabric from him? Well, here's my chance to pay him back.'

Ellen looked doubtful. She drummed her fingertips thoughtfully on the table. 'Hum, I see what you mean. Well, in that case perhaps you'd better go. We Fergusons don't believe in owing anything to any-one—especially to people like Morris Leslie. You've brought this situation upon yourself by your foolish-ness and you may as well suffer for it. It will teach you a lesson for the future.'

So breakfast was finished with no more than an occasional growl from Ellen and the exclamation, 'Cheek!' or 'Who does he think he is?' and Jane set off along the path to the main house.

She found Morris waiting for her in the library and went in a little shyly. 'So you've decided to come!' he greeted her.

'Yes, I—I felt I owed it to you,' she said awkwardly in an attempt to cover her happiness at the commis-sion, and could have bitten her tongue as she saw the result of her tactlessness.

'Owed it to me? I don't quite follow,' he said

coldly.

'I—I mean, you told me you'd look for repayment some day,' she stammered.

His brow wrinkled. Then instantly, to her relief, a smile flitted across his face. 'Oh, now I understand! You're repaying me for the material we bought in Aberdeen. Yes, you Fergusons have your pride, haven't you? You don't take anything without paying for it.' He was silent, then went on more thoughtfully, 'Perhaps it's not such a bad idea after all. Or at least we might say that while the Fergusons carry it too far, there are others one meets in life who don't have enough of the spirit.'

He gazed through the window for a long minute and she wondered what occasions of ingratitude in his life sprang to his mind at that moment. But she had no right to ask, she knew. The girl who lay upstairs in bed, her hand bandaged, was the one to whom he would reveal his secret heartaches.

She was taken aback when he asked, 'Tell me, do you regard this chore as merely a repayment? In other words, would you have refused to come this morning had there not been this question of a debt to be repaid?'

'You have no right to ask such questions!' she burst out after a moment.

There was a smile on his face as he said mischievously, 'I know I have no right, and yet I can't resist. Tell me, Jane, truthfully, would you have come?'

She was silent. How could she tell him of the happiness she felt at the thought of being able to do something for him? 'I'd have come all the same,' she told him.

'I'm glad to hear that,' he told her gravely, 'because

we Leslies have our pride too. We don't demand repayment of a favour unless we know that the person involved is anxious to do so. You see, we too always pay our way.'

Jane gave a little chortle of laughter. 'No wonder you and Aunt Ellen don't get along,' she exclaimed. 'You're too alike in character ever to see eye to eye about anything. Pride is clashing against pride, and you should really be at war.'

He grinned. 'Yes, perhaps that's what's wrong. You know, Jane, I have to admire that great-aunt of yours and somehow I feel in my bones that we'll come to an understanding finally. Believe me, how far away that date is depends solely upon her.'

As Jane took her place behind the typewriter and rolled in a sheet of paper, she felt a little glow of happiness. Somehow it meant a lot to her that Ellen should make her peace with Morris. Not that it would affect her own life, instantly the thought struck her. His concern on the previous evening when Rhoda had been hurt had shown her clearly who was the important woman in his future. As soon as Rhoda was up and about again, they would no doubt announce their engagement—and then— Then she herself would have to choose between going away from Kirtleside or remaining to witness his happiness in his marriage to another woman.

'Is that chair high enough for you?' he was asking. 'Rhoda's taller than you are.' As he spoke he handed her a cushion and arranged it on the seat for her.

For an instant before she began to take his dictation, Jane glanced around the library. Perched on her high seat behind the typewriter she was aware of every detail: the suits of armour against the walls, bibelots on the tables, the whiteness of the sheepskin rugs against the gleaming wood floor, the filing cabinets which had been introduced since Rhoda's arrival. It seemed a long time since that far distant afternoon when she had first seen this room and he had assumed that she had come for an interview in reply to his advertisement. Now, by a strange coincidence, she was acting as his secretary. It gave her a little glow of happiness as he began to stride up and down the room and dictate letters.

At first she was a little nervous. The typewriter seemed strange to her touch and she fumbled in trying to be over-hasty.

'Don't hurry! Let your fingers become accustomed to the machine,' he told her.

With this reassurance, she felt more at ease and soon became absorbed in the work.

After a while he went out, leaving her to check addresses, type envelopes, file the copy letters and make a note of phone calls.

In no time it was eleven o'clock and she was glad to sip the steaming hot coffee Mrs MacInnes had sent in to her.

When the maid returned to collect the cup and saucer, she brought a message from Rhoda asking if she would go up to her room for a few moments.

Jane stood up immediately and followed the girl upstairs in some trepidation. What had Rhoda to say to her? she wondered. The dreadful accusation that she had deliberately caused the accident seemed to ring through her mind and she could visualise only too clearly the white-faced, sobbing girl who had been carried up to her bed on the previous evening.

To her relief she found Rhoda sitting up in bed

wearing a beautiful bedjacket edged with swansdown. Her room was luxuriously furnished in pale Swedish furniture, with cool, clean lines that somehow seemed to suit the personality of the occupant. The decor, too, of pale grey with touches of chrome yellow and tomato red, seemed a fitting background for the hard, taut face of the girl who now fixed her with inimical eyes.

'I'm told you're typing letters for Morris,' she began without preamble, as soon as the maid had gone. 'So you've got what you wanted and sooner than I ever dreamed you would! But then you always had your eye on my job, hadn't you?'

'What do you mean?' gasped Jane.

'I mean the simple truth, that you seized your opportunity as soon as it arrived.'

'You—you're not referring to the accident?'

'Accident!' Rhoda sat up in bed. 'Do you dare to stand there and tell me it was an accident? You saw your chance and took it. You deliberately poured the boiling sauce over my hand, knowing it would put me out of action so that you could insinuate yourself into Windgates and set yourself up in my place. You'd do anything, wouldn't you, to get close to Morris, and show him how clever you are. Not that I think you'll be able to hold down the job! With all respect to you, my dear, good girl, I don't think you're as capable as I am. Morris will soon get tired of your bungling efforts. He's a man who likes efficiency, and if you thought to shine in his eyes, you'll find that you've only done yourself a disservice.'

'You don't really believe all this?' Jane said through stiff lips.

'Of course I believe it,' snapped Rhoda. 'What else

is there to believe? It's perfectly obvious, isn't it? Not that it will gain you anything. You can give up the chase after Morris, because I already have him hooked. Your trickery has turned back on yourself, and you've only thrown him into my arms. Look!'

As she spoke she flung out her bandaged hand and pointed towards the table beside her bed, upon which was an ornate basket of fruit, a selection of the latest paperbacks, and an expensive transistor radio which was softly playing music as a background to their conversation. 'These are from Morris, and he would have heaped gifts upon me, but I had sense enough to stop him.'

The energetic movement of Rhoda's bandaged hand had caught Jane's eye. 'You're not badly burned, are you, Rhoda?' she pleaded.

'What? What do you mean?' There was a belligerent note in Rhoda's voice.

'Gregory didn't seem to think that it was—was so bad,' Jane faltered, intimidated by the brilliant glare in Rhoda's eyes.

'And who's going to listen to Gregory?' blustered Rhoda. 'He'd rather go fishing any day than make a name for himself in medicine.'

'But the sauce *wasn't* boiling,' Jane persisted. 'I noticed that at the time. I was so relieved to think that it had cooled a great deal and—'

'And what?' Rhoda demanded. 'Just what are you implying?' But her eyes had dropped and unconsciously she was fiddling with her hair with the finger tips of her right hand which protruded at the end of the bandage. 'You're not suggesting that I'm malingering, are you?'

Suddenly Jane knew that this was just what Rhoda

was doing.

'You're not hurt nearly as bad as you're pretending,' she cried impulsively.

'And why should I do such a thing?' Rhoda asked evasively.

'I—I don't know,' Jane began. Then as her eyes fell once more upon that bedside table, laden with the gifts Morris had showered upon his secretary, she knew. 'You're doing it to win Morris's sympathy.'

'And what if I am?' Rhoda demanded. 'All's fair in love and war! Oh, the burn did hurt abominably at first, although I was lucky to get off more lightly than I expected. But I've learned that a man can grow tired of competence and independence. It does no harm for a woman to be a clinging vine at times. Morris is all concern about my welfare, and I must say I find it a refreshing change.' As she spoke she indicated a vase of freesia on a table at the end of her bed. 'He can't do enough to show me how much he cares,' she told Jane triumphantly.

Jane drew in a great breath of relief. The knowledge that Rhoda was not badly burned was balm to her, but she had spent a sleepless night worrying about this woman and she felt resentment rush through her at Rhoda's cool admission.

'How could you?' she asked indignantly. 'Do you realise how worried we've all been? Morris is truly concerned about you: he was terribly upset when it happened, and you put on a show of being in such dreadful suffering.'

'I've already told you that it was very painful at first,' Rhoda said coolly. 'I can assure you I was putting on no show then. But afterwards—well, I admit I didn't own up to the relief I felt when Gregory dressed it. Why should I? Remember, I'm a lone wolf in this world without as much as a devoted great-aunt to give a background to my life. I have to do the best I can for myself—and believe me, it's paid off in this instance.'

Jane drew in her breath with a gasp of annoyance. 'What if I were to go straight downstairs and tell Morris all this?' she demanded.

'Tell him what exactly?' asked Rhoda.

'That you're playing on his sympathies, and—'

Rhoda laughed softly. 'He wouldn't believe you, not for an instant! You're wasting your time threatening me. Besides, Morris would read your motive—he would know that you were just jealous of me and trying to put between us.'

In silence Jane stared into the other girl's triumphant face.

'Besides, now that you've arrived on the scene, you may not be surprised to hear that I shall put in an appearance at dinner this evening. I shall however be suitably pale and wan, you may be sure—the brave little woman getting to her feet and struggling downstairs in the teeth of affliction.'

Jane could feel her heart sink at this information. She had been looking forward to acting as Morris's secretary for some time. Now that would no longer be possible. There was no doubt that Rhoda had spoken only the truth when she had boasted that she was the more competent. Morris would hardly make do with her typing, once Rhoda was on her feet again.

'Don't look so cast-down,' Rhoda said mockingly. 'As far as I'm concerned you can have the run of the house for a few days longer. I've made so much fuss about this burn of mine that I simply daren't get back to work too soon.'

As Jane turned towards the door, Rhoda called softly, 'Count your hours alone with Morris, my dear girl, because they're shortly coming to an end—for good and all this time!'

Perhaps Rhoda was right, Jane thought that afternoon, as she poured tea for Morris in the library. She would make the best of these hours alone with him. It was good to be seated here with him, to pour tea for him, and to enjoy his conversation. If only this could be something permanent and not the passing dream of a moment, which she now knew it to be!

Later Morris asked Jane if she could possibly stay on for dinner and do a few more hours' typing before she went home.

She hesitated. Would Ellen be lonely in the factor's house as evening drew on? she wondered. Besides, in recent weeks she had worried a great deal about her great-aunt's health.

As if reading her thoughts, he said, 'If you're concerned about your great-aunt, I'll have Maggie call in this evening and sit with her.'

Jane gladly agreed to do this and immediately he made several phone calls to the village to make sure Maggie got the message and was willing to comply.

True to her intention, Rhoda joined them in the library just before dinner looking wan and interesting in a pale make-up which was emphasised by the black dress she had put on. The bandage on her right hand was snowy white against the darkness of her dress, showing only the finger tips with pearly nails.

Morris assisted her to a seat beside the fire in which a few logs were burning, for there was a slight chill in the evening air.

'Tell me, how does your hand feel now?' he asked solicitously.

'Really dreadful.' Rhoda leaned her head against the wing of her chair with a weary air. 'One doesn't like to complain and really I wouldn't have come down if I hadn't been so dreadfully bored. I'm quite helpless. It will be days before I'm able to use my fingers again. Such an unfortunate accident!' She glanced at Jane, then added pleasantly, 'Now don't think, Jane, that I'm blaming you in the slightest, but I must say I'm glad you feel sufficiently responsible to come here and try to assist while I'm out of things. Tell me, how are you getting along?'

'She's doing surprisingly well,' Morris told her, as he poured a drink and brought it to her. 'You'll have to look to your laurels, Rhoda. There's the makings of a very good secretary under that quiet exterior.'

'Oh, indeed!' Rhoda smiled sourly. She stretched out her right hand to take the glass from him, then quickly drew it back. 'Better put it here on my left, Morris,' she said, looking slightly confused.

He did as she bade him, then returned to his own place across the fire.

'Oh yes, Jane's doing very well,' he returned to the subject. 'In fact, I've asked her to have dinner here this evening so that we can put in a couple of extra hours afterwards. By that time we should have caught up with the backlog that's accumulated owing to the accident.'

There was a gathering tension in Rhoda's face as she listened to this and Jane could clearly see that she had assumed that the work would have fallen hopelessly behind when she herself was not there to oversee everything.

179

The gong sounded for dinner just then and as he stood up, Morris said casually, 'Oh, Rhoda, you're near the basket, would it be too much trouble to put a log on in case the fire burns low while we're at dinner?'

'No, of course not,' she said pleasantly, as she stooped and with her right hand picked up a thick log and pitched it easily into the fire. Then she stood up, smoothed down her dress and turned towards the door. It was only then that she seemed to become aware that both Jane and Morris were regarding her fixedly. It was plain that she had complete control of her fingers and that the action had cost her no pain.

In the lengthening silence Rhoda burst out, 'You did that deliberately, didn't you?'

'Yes,' he answered coolly. 'I was wondering just how badly you'd been injured, and now I know. It's plain that you're not as badly burned as you'd like us to think. I'm afraid you've been playing on our sympathies, Rhoda.'

'But why should I do such a thing?' she queried rather weakly. 'It did hurt abominably, Morris, and—'

As she spoke one of the maids appeared with the message that there was a phone call for Morris.

As soon as he had gone out Rhoda turned to Jane furiously. 'So you told him!' she cried.

'Told him what?' asked Jane.

'Don't pretend you don't know what I'm talking about. You told him the burn wasn't really bad. How else could he have known?'

'But I didn't,' Jane exclaimed. 'I wouldn't dream of doing such a thing, and—'

'Don't speak such nonsense,' interrupted Rhoda

furiously. 'You're wasting your time telling a pack of lies. Of course you told him. The opportunity was too good to be missed. But don't think you'll get away with it. I'll teach you that when you measure swords with me you've taken on more than you bargained for. I'll make sure Kirtleside has seen the last of you, once and for all!'

As she spoke she moved towards the door. 'You can tell Morris that I don't feel up to staying on for dinner. My hand is paining me too much. I'll just take a sedative and try to get some sleep.'

She went from the room with long, angry strides, leaving Jane staring after her.

What would Rhoda do now? she asked herself fearfully. She had learned to dread the ruthless self-absorption of the other woman and to know that there was nothing she would stop at when she was determined to get her own way.

When Morris returned to the library his first question was, 'Where's Rhoda?'

'She's gone to bed,' Jane told him.

'Her hand was too painful to permit her to stay up, no doubt,' he said sardonically. 'But don't look so troubled, Jane. After all, there is no need for you to worry any more, now we know that she's not really suffering.'

'It's not that,' Jane admitted. 'But she blames me for telling you that—that—'

'That she was malingering?' he finished.

'Well, yes,' Jane admitted.

'Such nonsense!' he returned. 'I can see for myself, can't I? Besides, I recollected Gregory Shields saying last night that the burn wasn't as bad as we'd feared, and after a while I began to put two and two together and to see how the land lay. If you remember, you said yourself that the sauce had cooled quite a bit, and when I thought about it I realised that Angus and I had strolled along the river bank for some distance before we turned back towards the grill. In fact, the sauce was certainly not boiling when the accident happened. Naturally I wanted to test her out. Rhoda can be too clever at times. Come along! We're having green pea and hambone soup this evening. No sense in letting Rhoda's antics spoil a good Scottish dish!'

But in the library once more, when dinner was over, Jane's attention was distracted. Her mind was filled with dread in connection with the threat Rhoda had made. What revenge would she take for what she was firmly convinced was a shrewd attempt on Jane's part to put between her and the man she loved so possessively?

As she made all sorts of stupid mistakes, Morris said in exasperation, ' Your mind's only half on your work, Jane, but then you've had a long, hard day. Better go off home now and have a good night's sleep. You'll feel more up to things in the morning. As to Rhoda, she'll undoubtedly need to rest for a few days more until her hand has healed properly.'

In the morning Jane felt much more optimistic: somehow, during the night, her fears of the previous evening seemed to have melted away. When Rhoda thought about it, Jane told herself, she would realise that it had not been with her assistance that Morris had seen through the ruse to win his sympathies. Anyway, in what possible way could Rhoda harm her? she asked herself. Now it was with Ellen's full consent that she was seeing Morris. The secretary might threaten and bluster, but there was really nothing she could do.

She dressed carefully, putting on the blue dress he had admired when she had worn it during their last trip to Aberdeen together. She brushed her hair until it shone and applied an extra touch of make-up. But she knew it was happiness at the thought of being in his company once more that brought a flush to her cheeks and a sparkle to her eyes.

She hurried along the broad path to the main house and found Morris waiting for her in the library.

'Congratulations,' he greeted her, 'you look rested this morning and efficient—but not too efficient, I'm glad to say.'

'I'm certainly not as efficient as Rhoda.' She perched herself on her high seat behind the typewriter, glad that her back was to him so that he might not see the happiness his approval gave her.

'You mustn't deprecate yourself,' he told her. 'You've done remarkably well. In your own way you're extremely competent. The difference is that with you it's unobtrusive. Maybe it's because you're so much younger and extreme youth is always appealing. It's unfair, perhaps—but there it is.' He broke off, then said briskly, 'But to get down to business! Now, let me see, where did we stop off yesterday—'

As he dictated memoranda, Jane found that this morning her fingers flew about the keys of the typewriter as if by magic. Now everything seemed easy and effortlessly she was able to keep up with the pace of his dictation.

At eleven they stopped for coffee and as Jane sipped the steaming cup and nibbled a biscuit, he said, 'I'll be out for the rest of the morning, but before I go I want to ask you an important question.'

' Yes?'

' What about the interiors of the remaining chalets? Are you prepared to design them?'

She placed her cup on the saucer with a little clatter and surveyed him, wide-eyed.

' Well?' he asked with a smile.

' I'd love that,' she said slowly. ' I've been wondering what you would do about the others and I simply didn't dare to hope that—'

' That I'd employ you? And why not? I couldn't choose a better person for the job.'

Slowly Jane picked up her cup once more. Over the rim her extraordinarily blue eyes were fixed on some vision that only she could see. How wonderful to be able to choose furniture and carpets, cushions and curtains to her heart's content, letting her artistic abilities have full play. Her next effort might be completely modern in tone—all bright shining surfaces with here and there a touch of deep black velvet to emphasise the brilliant clear colours—

' Jane, you're daydreaming again!' His voice broke into her thoughts.

' Only about the chalets,' she told him a little shyly.

' Well, no more dreaming this morning,' he told her laughingly as he went into the garden through one of the french windows which stood wide open to the lawns and shrubberies starred with blossom and filled with the sound of bird-song.

Left to herself, Jane set about typing fair copies of the letters and incorporating some alterations he had instructed her to make.

She was quite absorbed when there was a knock on the door and Mrs MacInnes came in. Her manner was distressed and immediately Jane knew that she was the bearer of bad news.

'Dr Shields is here and has asked to see you,' she began in a grave voice, on her face an expression of compassion.

'What—what is it?' Jane faltered. Immediately she was struck with the thought that something dreadful had happened to Ellen.

Mrs MacInnes glanced over her shoulder towards Gregory, who lingered in the doorway, and in a moment he was confirming Jane's worst fears. Ellen had collapsed, but managed to send for him and he, as soon as he had done what he could for her on the spot, had ordered her to be taken to hospital where she would have the benefit of all the latest equipment.

That was the bare story, but Jane drew in her breath with a gasp of dismay when she heard that Rhoda had been there at the time.

'So it was Rhoda who sent for you?' she asked in bewilderment.

'No, I'm afraid Rhoda left as soon as it happened. It was Maggie who phoned me, and when I questioned her about it she told me that she didn't know exactly what had taken place, but that Rhoda must have been with Ellen at the time. Maggie, in the kitchen, could hear their voices raised, and couldn't help overhearing a good deal of what was said. Apparently Rhoda was telling Ellen that you had attended the barbecue, for she distinctly heard Ellen denying that you had been there. It was a great mistake for you to go, Jane. You should have guessed Rhoda would make capital of it. She's crazy about Morris and I think she knows now that he doesn't really care for her, and you're in love with him—I see that clearly.'

But Jane wasn't listening. 'Take me to Aunt

Ellen,' she whispered, her face pale. How bitterly she reproached herself for putting this opportunity in Rhoda's hands to injure Ellen even further.

But Gregory's eyes were upon the wide windows standing open to the sunlit garden. Framed in them was Morris, and it was clear from his expression that he had already heard the news.

'Here's the man who'll drive you to the hospital, Jane,' Gregory was saying in a low voice that only she could hear. 'I know you're not in love with me and never will be. Morris is the man who has your thoughts and your heart.'

Without a backward glance he turned and strode towards the door. He was gone from the room and out of her life for ever, Jane knew, as Morris hurried towards her. In a moment his arms were about her and she was sobbing on his shoulder.

'Don't cry, Jane. It may not be as bad as you fear. I'll have the car brought around immediately and we'll go to see her.'

As they drove swiftly towards the hospital, Morris said quietly, 'You know, this is all my fault. You told me you didn't want to go to the barbecue, but I insisted. You were wiser than I, and I bitterly regret it now. But you see, I didn't understand Rhoda's character. It didn't occur to me that she would be malicious enough to upset Ellen by telling her you were there.'

'I think she's in love with you, Morris,' Jane told him.

'And I'm in love with you.'

They had no chance of speaking further, because now his powerful car was moving along the wide hospital avenue.

Very shortly they were told by a severe-looking nurse that they might see Ellen for a few minutes.

Jane crept into her great-aunt's room on tip-toe, to find Ellen sitting up in bed sipping a cup of tea.

She didn't hide her delight in seeing her looking so much better than she had expected.

'Oh, there's life in this old warhorse yet,' Ellen told her gruffly. 'Everyone here is amazed at the improvement I've made already. I'm one of the wonders of the world, it seems. But tell me, how did you get here so soon?'

Jane looked at her apprehensively. Dared she tell Ellen that it was Morris who had brought her?

'I suppose you've been with that Morris fellow again,' Ellen remarked. 'After all, you have to do his typing to repay your debt, haven't you?'

'Yes, he drove me here to see you,' Jane faltered.

'In that case you'd better ask him to come in,' Ellen said. 'It isn't civil to leave him outside without as much as offering him a cup of tea.'

As Jane hesitated, eyeing her great-aunt rather apprehensively, Ellen went on, 'Go on, girl, I shan't eat him, you know.'

So Jane went to the door and whispered to Morris, 'She wants you to come in.'

As soon as she saw him, Ellen called out in a surprisingly loud, clear voice, 'Do come in and shut the door. There's a draught, you know—always is in hospitals.'

So Morris came in and as soon as he was seated she tackled him, 'It seems you drove Jane to visit me, and for that I must thank you. But if you're sufficiently interested in her welfare you can now drive the pair of us back home immediately.'

Even Morris's usually impassive face showed something like alarm at this suggestion. 'But you're getting the best care here,' he told her placatingly. 'Everything is being done to get you on your feet as soon as possible.'

'And have you any idea of what all this is going to cost?' Ellen demanded. 'I've been making inquiries and it seems this is one of the most expensive private units in the world.'

'What of it?' he returned. 'If that's what's bothering you, put it out of your mind right away. The fees will be met, you may be sure of that.'

'Not by you, I hope!' Ellen told him tartly.

'No, by yourself! You know very well I never wished you to pay any rent for the factor's house.'

'Yes, but I did so,' Ellen exclaimed proudly. 'All my life I've been an independent woman—and I'll be independent to the end.'

'Well, your independence is paying off now,' he told her, 'because I put the money you insisted on giving me for the rent into a separate account and it's there for you to meet your own fees, so you can lie back and relax and enjoy your expensive treatment.'

There was a silence after this and it was clear that Ellen was having a tussle with herself. 'You know, Morris, I've had a very poor opinion of you,' she said at last, 'but I'm forced to revise my ideas. I've been pig-headed and obstinate and I admit it. So there!'

Jane, listening, was thinking that it was no wonder these two had taken so long to come to an understanding. So much alike in their strong and obstinate temperaments it was inevitable that they should clash! However, time had taught them to respect each other.

Her thoughts were interrupted as Ellen said abruptly, 'You know, Jane, you could do worse than take him!'

Jane gave a gasp of surprise, then said softly, 'But he hasn't asked me, Aunt Ellen.'

'Well, I'm asking you now,' Morris said immediately. 'Will you marry me, Jane?'

Jane looked at him, her love shining in her eyes, but somehow she couldn't find words to reply. While she swallowed the lump in her throat, Ellen said sharply, 'Well, speak up, girl. You've just been asked a civil question.'

'Yes, Morris, I will,' Jane told him, almost in a whisper.

As they gazed across the room at each other, Ellen looked from one to the other sharply. 'Well, isn't it customary to seal the bargain with a kiss?'

When Morris had obediently kissed Jane lightly on the lips, Ellen leaned back on her pillows. 'I don't consider that much of a kiss,' she remarked. 'We used to do much better when I was a girl. However, I suppose you'll do better later on. Now off you go and leave me to have a good sleep. I need it after the excitement of today.'

As they strolled through the hospital grounds hand in hand Jane said happily, 'Aunt Ellen is going to be all right.'

'Yes,' he told her. 'There's a happy future ahead for her—and for us too, Jane. You know, in many ways, she's a wise woman. She was right in saying our kiss was very unsatisfactory. Now here's a shady rose pergola. No one's around and I think we should seal our bargain with a real kiss, a long one this time, long enough to last us until the end of our lives.'

FREE! Harlequin Romance Catalogue

Here is a wonderful opportunity to read many of the Harlequin Romances you may have missed.

The HARLEQUIN ROMANCE CATALOGUE lists hundreds of titles which possibly are no longer available at your local bookseller. To receive your copy, just fill out the coupon below, mail it to us, and we'll rush your catalogue to you!

Following this page you'll find a sampling of a few of the Harlequin Romances listed in the catalogue. Should you wish to order any of these immediately, kindly check the titles desired and mail with coupon.

To: **HARLEQUIN READER SERVICE, Dept. N 309**
M.P.O. Box 707, Niagara Falls, N.Y. 14302
Canadian address: Stratford, Ont., Canada

☐ Please send me the free Harlequin Romance Catalogue.

☐ Please send me the titles checked.

I enclose $＿＿＿＿＿ (No C.O.D.'s), All books are 60c each. To help defray postage and handling cost, please add 25c.

Name ＿＿＿＿＿＿＿＿＿＿＿＿＿＿＿＿＿＿＿＿＿

Address ＿＿＿＿＿＿＿＿＿＿＿＿＿＿＿＿＿＿＿

City/Town ＿＿＿＿＿＿＿＿＿＿＿＿＿＿＿＿＿

State/Prov. ＿＿＿＿＿＿＿＿＿＿＿＿ Zip＿＿＿＿

Have You Missed Any of These

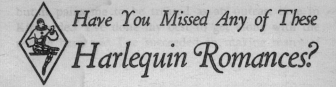

Harlequin Romances?